RACKETS, INC.

Borgo Press Books by JOHN GLASBY

The Dark Boatman: Tales of Horror and the Cthulhu Mythos
The Lonely Shadows: Tales of Horror and the Cthulhu Mythos
The Mystery of the Crater: A Science Fiction Novel
Rackets, Inc.: A Johnny Merak Classic Crime Novel (#1)

RACKETS, INC.

A JOHNNY MERAK CLASSIC CRIME NOVEL, BOOK ONE

JOHN GLASBY

THE BORGO PRESS
MMXIII

RACKETS, INC.

FIRST BORGO PRESS EDITION

Published by Wildside Press LLC

www.wildsidebooks.com

RACKETS, INC.

CONTENTS

CHAPTER ONE
DEATH AND A LADY

I guess it was to be the kind of arrival in the country that Maxie had always planned. After all, he had been away for seven years, and maybe he thought that if he came straight in on the normal air service from Mexico City to Los Angeles, he'd throw most of the sharks wide of the scent. There were plenty of them still around, even after seven years, but the majority of them would be expecting him to sneak in like the rat he was.

Maybe they didn't have the kind of connections I had. Maybe they even figured there would be plenty of time once he did arrive because, big as Los Angeles is, there's no place for even a rat to hide if the Big Boys are after your blood.

In the old days Maxie had been the principal owner of a string of motels scattered throughout the coastal resorts south of Los Angeles, with a share in plenty of other interests, all of them strictly legal and above board. But he had always been one of the kingpins of the Underworld Organisation until he had crossed them up seven years ago and skipped over the border.

Now they were waiting for him, somewhere, ready to take everything they could lay their hands on once they caught up with him. They'd take his money and his women and then give him the once-over, just for laughs.

In the end he wouldn't be Big Maxie anymore. Just a has-been who'd made two fatal mistakes: double-crossing the Organisation in the first place and then coming back, looking for trouble instead of playing it safe and staying where he was.

A man cannot walk away from the Organisation after spitting right in their faces and hope to stay in one piece for long. Maxie Temple was somewhere on that plane coming in to land, and within minutes he'd be stepping off and walking into trouble. Big trouble.

But maybe he knew all this and had his own plans. Not only for himself but for the Organisation also. The thought made me uneasy.

I slipped my hand into my pocket, closed my fingers around the .38, and tried to make myself look inconspicuous. A gun was easy to get, but its possession was, of course, a felony. But I'd had this particular weapon for seven years. There was little chance of it being traced back to me if anything went wrong.

A little nagging thought was nibbling at the edge of my mind and I forced myself to concentrate on it, to bring it out into the open. There was a man standing by the newsstand, a paper between his hands, hiding his face almost entirely. Once or twice he seemed to be glancing unobtrusively in my direction.

The fourth or fifth time it happened, I turned my head slightly and paid some attention to him. There was nothing out of the ordinary about him at first sight. He was just a type.

You find his class nearly everywhere. Square-framed, a wide-brimmed soft hat pulled well down over his eyes, shading the upper half of his features. A clipped moustache over thin lips that were clamped into a tight, hard line. A special type of man, when looked at more closely. A hoodlum of the lowest breed. And there was no need for me to think twice about the reason for him being there at that particular time and in that particular place. He lowered his paper as he caught me watching him, then sauntered over.

"Waiting for somebody?" He stood square and straight, eyes faintly amused, looking at me, hoping I'd start something, ready for a fight.

I swung round and looked into his narrowed eyes. "Who the hell are you?"

There was no doubt in my mind that he was somebody who knew me and had probably been tipped off as to why I was there myself, but I didn't recognise him at the moment. There must have been thousands like him in Los Angeles wandering from bar to bar, doing dirty work for the Big Boys, sweeping aside those minor crooks who happened to be in the way of the Organisation.

And it looked as though a few of the big shots were moving in already. Rolling forward with the irresistible quality of some giant steamroller to smash Big Maxie and everything he stood for, utterly and completely. But first they'd have their play with him.

"You're Johnny Merak, aren't you?" he said, speaking between his teeth. "My guess is that you're here to get Maxie Temple, right?"

"What's that got to do with you?" I asked. I didn't know the hoodlum, but he sure knew plenty about me, and if there wasn't to be any hitch in my plans, I'd have to get to know what his particular game was.

"You came down here from uptown less than an hour ago. Your car's parked a couple or so blocks from here. Seven years ago you were in on the big deals with Maxie before he hit out for Mexico City. Since then you have been up on a three-year stretch in Big Q for something Maxie framed up, just to keep you out of the way. Now you want to get even with him, maybe even try to clear yourself. That's the way of it, isn't it?" There was something ugly about his face as he thrust it up to mine.

"Well, I'll be dammed," I said softly.

"You will be if you don't make yourself scarce, bud." He licked his lips impatiently with a dry hunger. "We don't want you in on this deal. That clear?"

"Just who is it you're working for?"

"Could be we're both working for the same people, only they've just decided not to trust you."

"You're lying in your teeth, punk," I muttered thickly. "I work for nobody but Johnny Merak. Tell your bosses that. And I'm not scared off so easily."

He laughed. An ugly sound. "I was just waiting for

you to say that. The guys I'm working for don't want anything to go wrong. Maybe you're just a little man, but they seem to think that you might be able to louse up this deal, so I'm here to keep an eye on you. They wouldn't want you to do anything stupid."

I guessed what was coming next. Land yourself into something dirty and you're bound to run into people who're the same. You can't expect anything else. We were almost alone now. A couple of guys were standing in the main entrance to the lounge, but they were looking intently the other way. They obviously didn't want any trouble, I decided.

This fellow would be a dirty fighter, I'd figured, hoping to cripple within seconds, stiffened fingers in the eyes, all his weight behind a swift punch to the belly and no holds barred. All these little thoughts had been running through my brain while we had been talking.

Before he could move, I reached over, wrapped my fingers tightly around his left wrist, pulled his arm so that his head went well down, slipped my other arm swiftly under his downstretched elbow, across the back of his neck, then pressed. Turning him swiftly, my right knee came up and hit him hard in the pit of the stomach. His breath gushed out in a single, agonised bleat and he made funny whistling noises as he tried to suck in air.

There was a gun in his pocket. I could feel it as I swung his body towards me sharply. So they hadn't been kidding. They were playing for keeps, meaning to get rid of me if I didn't play ball. Hell, I thought, they must want to get hold of Maxie pretty badly.

Before the hoodlum could recover his bounds, I dropped his hand and hit him twice with my bunched fist. Once to the heart, then on the tip of his square jaw. If it hadn't been for the urgency, I might not have been quick enough to get rough like that.

One usually thinks twice about roughing up the hirelings of the Big Men, and there were lots of things twisting inside me—Maxie, my last chance to clear myself, the power of the Organisation moving in relentlessly. It was no time for an unknown hoodlum to start getting fresh with Johnny Merak.

Apart from the gasp as I hit him in the belly, he hadn't made a sound. His face was a dirty grey and there was blood on his lips where his teeth had bitten deeply into them. He was still groggy as I slipped my hand into his pocket and brought out the gun. It was a German automatic. A big weapon for these men. Usually they preferred to carry small, easily hidden weapons.

"You'll regret this, Merak," he mumbled, wiping his lips. I shoved him back against the wall. Still no suspicious move from the two characters near the lounge.

"Shut up!" I said. "I'm in no mood for arguing." I looked at the automatic, then placed it carefully in my pocket. "I'll keep this," I said, "just in case you start to get any fresh ideas. Now get moving."

"Is this your last answer, Merak?"

"Get moving," I repeated. "And if I ever see you again, I'll finish the job."

He opened his mouth to say something more and I hit him again, hard, with my fist. His head snapped back and there was a glint of pure evil in his close-set eyes. Steadying himself, he hung on to the wall for a couple of seconds, shaking his head. Then he rubbed his jaw tenderly.

"I'll remember that," he said ominously, and then walked away. I watched him stagger for a couple of paces, turn, and look back at me over his shoulder. Then he straightened himself and walked away, down the steps, and out into the street.

I walked into the lounge with long, quick steps, disregarding the fear that cut through my mind. It was all right acting tough in front of such hoodlums, but there was a fear all the same. You can't defy the Underworld and hope to get away with it forever. Your only chance is to get things done, the important things, before they finally catch up with you.

My watch showed nine-thirty. In five minutes the plane from Mexico City would be touching down and Big Maxie would have arrived, if everything had gone according to plan. And I had to get to him first, before the sharks got their teeth into him, spilling his gold and his blood.

Dead—and he was no use to me. And in the hands of the Big Boys he was as good as dead. I wondered with a little part of my mind what the hoodlum was doing at that particular moment. Reporting back—or watching me from some dark corner, biding his time, nursing his revenge?

Three men and a woman sat at a round table, all of them with glasses in front of them. They stopped talking as I walked past. One of the men whispered something and the woman turned her head to follow me.

There was something in her dark eyes that intrigued me. A smouldering, fathomless fire that seemed to burn right at the back of them. It was as if a hidden devil had suddenly jumped up from the black depths, licked its lips hungrily, then fallen back again. She had half-swung round and was toying with her glass idly.

Dark eyes, long black hair, curling over bare shoulders, and small, white teeth showing evenly because she was smiling a little with her lips just parted.

She was probably just curious about me. Maybe one of her guys knew me or had heard of me. There were a lot of things that could make a woman curious.

The loudspeaker system suddenly blared, catching my attention, directing it from the woman. She looked away and I could see that she was still smiling.

I shrugged. Women were a dime a dozen in Los Angeles. Shark-eyed girls from the studios of Hollywood, down for laughs, away from the cameras and television networks. They were good for laughs, too, if you had that kind of money, but that was about all.

I went outside and waited for the plane to come in. She was up there, somewhere, circling the airport. The wind was cool and there was a moon, low down, hiding behind strips of tattered cloud. A crowd was already there, jostling, talking loudly, looking at the long rows of lights that marked the runway.

Johnny Merak, I thought fiercely, you're a chump. Fancy thinking you can step in and cheat the Big Boys out of this deal. There will be some of them around, waiting. Why does a man have to try to make an idiot out of himself? To prove something? Seven long, waiting years—and now this. I found myself thinking suddenly about that woman at the table.

The half-open lips and the searing, naked passion in the dark eyes. A private hell with nothing at the bottom of it. Only devils that had to be kept chained and could never be quietened for long. Demanding and insistent.

But there had been something uncertain about her smile, too; so she wasn't quite as sure of herself as she would have liked to be. I reached down and felt the .38 resting snugly in my pocket, ready for any emergency.

I stood there, apart, on the edge of the crowd, and looked straight into the night with the brilliant light stretching away into the dipping distance. The plane was coming in gently, touching down with a distant bleat of protesting tyres. A moment later I could see it, then it vanished again into the darkness at the far end of the runway, and the urgent tension in my brain started piling up again.

How does a man get to be like Johnny Merak? For me it had been easy once I'd started on the slide. Everything connected with the racket seems big and exciting when you're only eighteen and a bit. You do it in the beginning because all the other kids do it;

because you want to get one step ahead of them all and stay that way.

The Big Men all have a decent, respectable front. They own large slices of real estate, chains of motels in the best quarters of town. Solid, dependable citizens. But at the back of it all, behind the pasteboard and the lies and the campaigning, you find the large and profitable rackets.

All the time there was trouble. Rival syndicates, people with bright ideas. That was why these men at the top needed others who could be trusted to carry out orders, to do the dirty work, and ask no questions. In the beginning I liked it fine. There were plenty of trips to the coast, the best hotels, and the bills were always paid by somebody you never saw.

The tough thing, though, is when it really hits you between the eyes and you see what a mess you've let yourself into. But then it's too late. Maxie had been the last of the big names as far as Johnny Merak was concerned. Anything rotten enough, anything the other boys wouldn't touch with a ten-foot pole, and I'd be the guy to fix it.

And in the end I had fixed myself so good that I still couldn't get out of the mess. Hence the gun and the meeting I intended to have with Maxie Temple. There were some pretty important papers he still had in his possession with Johnny Merak's name scrawled legibly across the bottom. If they got into the wrong hands, I'd go up the river for a far longer stretch than three years. And Maxie knew it.

Everybody knew it.

I watched the plane come in, propellers just ticking over.

A couple of overalled guys ran out the wheeled stairs and push them up against the door. I waited for it to open. The minute Maxie stepped off that plane and through the Customs, I wanted him. I wanted him bad.

The first passenger alighted, followed by three others. The fifth was Big Maxie. Seven years had changed him very little. Expensive clothes, a thick cigar, broad fleshy features, blue-eyed and smiling as though he hadn't a care in the world. Outwardly, he looked a regular guy. When you got to know him, you realised the evil that lay at the back of that genial mask.

A cold-blooded killer. It was like mistaking a man-eating tiger for a Persian cat. He walked forward slowly, eyes flicking from side to side looking for trouble, ready to meet it when it came. He seemed wary. And he had every reason to. For all he knew, his little game had come unstuck and half the crooks in Los Angeles were waiting for him behind the barrier to square accounts.

Maybe he thought he was still one of the top guns. His coming here like this must have meant that all hell was breaking loose south of the border. Ten yards away I saw him look up and stared directly at me. The look in his small eyes was one of surprise rather than fear. Then he looked away again and it was done deliberately. He knew me at first sight, but he was making it clear that he had dismissed me as unimportant. He was Maxie Temple, Big Shot.

But as far as I was concerned, in dismissing me he was making one of the biggest mistakes of his life.

I felt my fingers bite into the palm of my left hand. Maxie walked slowly with a small crowd of passengers, his face hard. He was puzzled. My being there was something he hadn't expected. It was something he was trying to figure out.

I suppose you know what you're doing, Johnny, I thought quickly. *Because if you don't, this could be the end of the line for you.*

Five minutes later Maxie came out of the Customs, walking hurriedly in a crush of people. Obviously, he'd been clever and arrived with a clean bill of health.

I saw him watching me furtively, like a rat in a corner. Perhaps he'd had second thoughts about me during those five minutes. It did something to me inside to see that first, faint touch of cringing fear. He would probably never understand how much I hated his guts.

Quite suddenly, without warning, his gaze flicked over my shoulder to something behind me and I knew then that trouble was going to break. It came sooner than I had expected. I half-turned my head, but by that time it was too late. Out of the corner of my eye I saw the black circular hole that appeared like a shadow between Maxie's eyes, the vacant look on his fleshy face as he sagged slowly, awkwardly, at the knees and hit the ground.

Whoever had shot him had used a silencer. A blind man could figure that, but by the time I had recovered from my surprise there was a crowd running forward, jostling each other, and it would have been like looking for the needle in the proverbial haystack to pick out his murderer.

Somewhere a woman began to scream in a high-pitched, hysterical voice.

I had known what I was risking when I had come to the airport. My record was known to the cops of perhaps a dozen states, also my sworn determination to fix Maxie Temple. Somehow, desperately, I had hoped to get to him in time to figure out a way of clearing myself. Now, he was dead, less than five yards from where I was standing like some dumb fool, and at any moment there would be a dozen cops milling around the joint and Johnny Merak would be picked up on suspicion.

I thought about that .38 in my pocket and decided I had better get out of the vicinity while I still had the chance. Awkward questions might be asked, and another thought occurred to me as I started to push my way through the crowd.

There were a lot of people who might want Maxie Temple out of the way permanently. There were also plenty who wanted Johnny Merak silenced for good, too. And maybe some clever guy had hit on the bright idea of doing both with the one shot.

The more I thought about it, the more likely it seemed. Ten to one that shot which killed Maxie Temple had come from a .38 similar to that in my pocket. And on top of that, another ten to one shot that somebody was, at that very moment, phoning for the cops, telling them that I had been spotted in the vicinity and I began to see what kind of a trap I'd let myself in for.

To Johnny Merak, the big thing now was to get as far away from the airport in as little time as possible. I ran down the steps outside three at a time. No sign of the square-shouldered hoodlum who had tried to be funny earlier. Maybe he was still around somewhere, reporting back on my movements, just in case I managed to slip through the police net.

Two blocks and I was nearly there. A siren was wailing dismally like a lost soul somewhere in the street ahead, coming nearer. A moment later three cars came cutting through the late-night traffic. Cars and trucks pulled out of the way, gliding into the kerb as they heard the wail of the sirens.

They went on past and I was beginning to feel better, more easy in my mind. For the time being I'd slipped the net and was still on the loose. Maxie was dead and there was nothing I could do to bring him back again.

I cursed the unknown assailant who had beaten me to him. That bullet which had cut into Maxie's brain and ended his life had ended my hopes of getting back those all-important papers that would have cleared me.

I turned the corner of the third block. My car was still there parked against the kerb, ready for a quick get-away. Eyes alert, I began to accelerate my stride. Once I was well away, there would be plenty of time to think things out, to plan the next move, pick up old threads, and see if any of them tied together to give me a new lead. If they didn't, I was right back where I had started, four years before.

I was still twenty or thirty yards from the car when I spotted them. Two or three dark shapes huddled in one of the doorways. That made me stop. They hadn't seen me yet, but they were waiting for me. They knew it was my car and I'd need it to get back into town.

I backed against the wall, stood there and waited. Maybe I could fight these three hoodlums waiting for me, but even if I did, the Organisation was so big that a dozen others could pop up out of the walls and hustle me off, and nobody would be any the wiser.

I thought of going back, hailing a cab. Uncertainly, I stepped away from the shadows. A long, sleek car pulled up suddenly against the side of the kerb, opposite to me. The door opened.

I swung round, my hand in my pocket. Then I stopped.

She was sitting there, behind the wheel, alone.

"Quickly! Get inside!" she said. Her voice was soft and husky, as I'd known it would be.

And that little devil was there again, leaping at the back of her coal-black eyes.

CHAPTER TWO
THE LADY SAYS YES

I slipped in beside her, and we pulled away into the mainstream of traffic. I turned my head and looked at her. She still seemed a trifle uncertain, not sure whether she had done the right thing or not.

"You know, you could be letting yourself in for a lot of trouble doing this for me," I said quietly. We were past the three lurking shadows and they had made no move, so I guess they hadn't spotted the switch.

"I always seem to do foolish things on the spur of the moment," she answered. There was an odd edge of strength to her voice and a quiet, dependable determination. A woman who could be trusted whenever the going got a little tough, I decided. But all that was only for the right guy. Not just anybody like Johnny Merak.

"How did you guess I was in trouble?"

"Oh, that." She laughed a little. "I was watching you back there at the airport. You didn't look like a man who'd come down to meet an old friend. You were after that man who was killed, weren't you?"

She looked at me out of the corner of her eye, eyeing me up and down in a way that made me feel hot inside.

"You seem to know quite a lot," I said cautiously. "Just where do you fit in on this deal?"

It struck me then that, apart from the obvious strength of character, this woman had a certain direct interest in my affairs. And that could mean trouble for both of us.

She didn't answer that one, not that I'd really expected her to, so I said: "What about those three guys you were with at the airport? They're tailing us right now, I suppose."

I must have sounded pretty bitter, because she took her eyes off the road for an instant to look round at me.

Then she shook her head. "I don't want to pry into your affairs, but you looked like a guy who could do with a break. I know you didn't shoot that man back there. But if you don't want to trust me, get out and walk the rest of the way, wherever it is you're going."

She slowed the car and edged in towards the kerb. There was no anger in her voice, nothing at all.

"Steady," I said, holding her arm. "Don't get sore. This is nothing personal. But I'm in a spot where I can't trust anybody. Not even a dame who happens to be in the right place at the right time. There's always something about that set-up that smells."

"Shall we say I was interested then. You're Johnny Merak, aren't you? It's all right. I got your name from one of the men who was with me back there. They seemed to know a lot about you."

"Yeah. I bet they did."

She clamped her lips tightly together and concentrated on driving for several minutes before speaking. "They said you'd worked for this man, Maxie Temple, before—when he was still one of the big shots in Los Angeles. Was that true?"

I nodded, feeling like a heel.

"And the rest of it?"

"He framed me before he got out of the country. Left me holding everything. I was sent up for three years. I swore then I'd pay him back for that."

"That's why you were at the airport tonight?"

"Partly. I knew he was supposed to be coming in on that plane. I didn't want to kill him, not there. He had something I wanted. I needed him alive to clear me. Now it's all finished, unless I can get some other lead."

"Such as what?"

"Find out who killed Maxie Temple—and why. Then get the truth from his killer."

"They'll be watching your place by now," she said coldly.

I hadn't thought of that particular angle. It was true, of course. They would be taking no chances now. I'd slipped through their fingers once too often. They'd have to pick me up now, unless the cops did it first. And when *that* happened, there'd be a murder rap hanging over me so watertight that even a blind D.A. would be able to send me up for the big burn.

If they wanted me, either way, they had me cold.

"Where do you figure on spending the night, Johnny?" She looked at me again out of the corner of her eyes.

"I'll find somewhere, I guess."

"Care to come up to my place?"

I watched her carefully. Maybe I went there, trusting, and there would be a couple of hirelings waiting behind the door, ready to pick me off. Things were happening too nicely for it to be anything but a fix. The big fix— and I was right in the middle of it. I could even feel it beginning to close in on me.

But what was the other alternative? Wandering around the dives in the east end of town. Haunting the bars, an easy target for any mobster on the prowl. I decided to take the risk.

"Sure. I'll string along with you."

I said it for response, hoping to find out more than I already knew, or guessed.

"My name is Dawn Grahame. I live a few blocks from here. You'll be all right there."

We were in the better quarter of Los Angeles. She looked like a dame with plenty of dough. Maybe I'd done her an injustice. Maybe she was the type who tagged onto a man when he was down, helping to get him back onto his feet again, getting a short kick out of watching him fight his way back to the top.

She cut a corner dangerously close, guided the car into the side. The house was in darkness, a two-story building of stone and redbrick, standing a little way back from the road. There was a garden of some kind in front of it, but in the darkness I couldn't see much of it. The moon was a thin crescent, riding the clouds, high. I got out and heard her close the other door quietly behind her.

Nearly ten-thirty. I shrugged my shoulders. They would still be looking for me. Men like Clancy Snow and Dutch McKnight. For four years I tried to keep away from contact with men like that. You couldn't fight them, really.

They are right in the background, behind the spider-webs of hoodlums and hirelings who took orders from above and worked you over good, so that you ended up crippled and maimed. Los Angeles was full of men who'd tried to defy the Organisation and lived to regret it.

My lighter flamed and I lit a cigarette, drawing the smoke gratefully into my lungs. There were a lot of things I had to straighten out inside me. For the moment I was safe. They would search the nightspots down-town first. Then they'd come uptown, never giving up.

One thing I knew without hesitation. The big men in L.A. would carry out their threats. They had got Maxie Temple within minutes of stepping off the plane. They'd had to stop him. If he'd lived and somehow made a comeback, their positions, individually, wouldn't have been worth a damn.

Then I followed Dawn up the white steps into the quiet porch and forgot about the Big Men of Los Angeles for a while. Somewhere, back in the early years, there had been a house like this for me, and the memory must have stayed with me somewhere, throughout the years, because I found I had never really lost it.

She stopped outside the door, took her key from her

bag and unlocked. We went inside, closing it gently behind us.

"I'll get you a drink," she said. "You look as though you could use one."

"Straight bourbon," I replied. "That'll suit me fine."

The drink was fine. Somehow I began to feel good, more relaxed than before.

"You'll be all right here." She sat down opposite me and leaned back. Her eyes followed me up and down. "Nobody's likely to drop around."

"What about your three friends?" I asked with a touch of irony.

"They won't come here. Not tonight, anyway."

She watched me with that sparkling friendliness, her dark eyes softer than before, with that unfathomable mystery at the back of them. A man could get lost in them, I thought, but that wasn't for me. Not yet. There were other, more important things to be taking care of.

Otherwise, Johnny Merak would find himself up to the neck in a murder rap and other things beside.

I took off my coat and shirt, pulled off my shoes, and took the soft blanket she handed to me before lying on the couch. While she was in the other room, I slipped the .38 from my pocket and pushed it beneath the pillow. No point in taking any chances. The heavy German automatic I'd taken from the hoodlum I unloaded and left in my pocket.

"You all right, Johnny?" Her voice reached me through the open doorway.

"Sure. I'm fine."

"Good night, Johnny."

There was a strange loneliness in her voice. I closed my eyes and there came the soft click of a door closing somewhere at the back of my consciousness.

It was the morning when I opened my eyes again. A grey light was spreading out of the east, lighting the objects in the room with a kind of halo. I got up, quietly, wondering where Dawn was. She came in a minute later with coffee.

"I thought you'd be up early," she said, placing it on the small table in the centre of the room.

The meal was one of silences, soon over. All the way through it she looked at me patiently, as if wondering why I did the things I did. Finally, she asked the question that had obviously been bothering her and it was a tough one.

"Would you really have killed that man last night, if you'd had the chance, Johnny?"

I thought a minute, and then decided not to lie to her. Time enough for that when I had to. "Yes," I said. "I'd have killed him. He deserves everything he got. If there was anything dirty to be done, Maxie Temple was in it up to the neck, close to the dirt."

"You must have known him well in the old days to have hated him so much." There was no accusation in her voice.

"Sure. I knew him. Now that he's dead, I'll have to kill the others. It can't be done any other way."

"But why, Johnny? You want to go through life with a dozen murder charges hanging over your head—running from the police, waiting for the other mobsters to catch up with you in some stupid, senseless vendetta?"

"I guess it'll have to be that way. Ever seen a rat when he's cornered? Well, take a good look at one now, while you've got the chance."

"I don't understand, Johnny."

"I thought I'd finished with dirty deals, Dawn. I thought maybe I could get out and turn into something decent and respectable. But I can't. These men like Clancy Snow and Dutch McKnight, they're rotten to the core."

A low voice saying big things, but the brain knowing full well that I lacked the courage or the ability to carry them out.

"But why do you have to take all the risks, get yourself beaten up and shot up?"

"I'm the only one who can do it, don't you see? There's blood on my shadow already. Maxie's blood. They've got me framed so tight I can't wriggle out. Maxie's gone, but I'm still around. They won't leave it to the cops to pick me up, that would be too uncertain. They'll come looking for me themselves. Now I have to get out of here. Maybe you don't know how they treat women. I do."

"They don't scare me." Her face was uplifted towards mine, her eyes shining as they had the night before.

"No, I guess you don't scare so easily," I said. There was a quick, deep look. She came to me quietly, put her arms around me, lifting her mouth to mine. That was when I really found her, and it was like nothing I had ever known before.

"Do you realise how powerful these people really are I'm trying to fight?" I asked. "Do you know that they'd cut your pretty face into little ribbons and laugh while they were doing it?"

"It's odd," she said quietly. "You seem to be more concerned about me than I am myself." She smiled. "I know them. I've met their type before and they don't frighten me." Her mouth twisted in contempt.

"Don't underestimate them, Dawn. Never do that." I was deadly serious.

Dawn looked at me, her eyes deep and black, her lips half-open. Her face was without expression.

"What do you intend to do?"

"There's only one way of meeting trouble," I said, "and that's halfway. No sense in running away from it. That's what I've been doing ever since Maxie left. The first thing I've got to do is get a lead of some kind. There must have been somebody who saw what happened last night."

"Do you think they'll talk? Especially to you."

"I'll find some way of making them," I said seriously, and meant it. Time was running out for me.

"Take my car, if you like," said Dawn, placing her hand on my arm. "But watch yourself." She went over to the window overlooking the street, pulled back the curtain gently and peered out.

"Anybody there?" I asked pointedly.

She shook her head. "The street looks deserted.

Nobody in sight."

I drank another cup of coffee, found a half-full bottle of whiskey in the small kitchen, and had that best of all morning drinks.

The little thoughts in my mind had a final chance to scamper around my brain as I made my way down the garden path and slid myself behind the wheel of Dawn's car. Usually, girls like Dawn Grahame don't act this way towards strangers, particularly a man with a record like mine. There was something more behind it. Something I meant to find out as soon as the opportunity presented itself.

CHAPTER THREE
THE BLIND ALLEY

I turned the ignition key, pushed the starter. The car was warm-hearted and started up immediately with a sudden whir of power. She slid forward easily, and the last glimpse of Dawn I had was a slight figure out the window waving her hand a little uncertainly. Then I turned the car into the street and headed downtown.

Ahead of me there was nothing but trouble, and behind me nothing but a lifetime of bitterness and regrets. A hell of a way to start the day.

The flashy bars in the east end of town would be open even at this early hour, and many of them well patronised. Perhaps there I might be able to pick up some shred of information, which would give me the lead I needed so desperately.

Frenchie's was open and busy as I drew up alongside the kerb. I threw a swift glance up and down the street before climbing out of the car. A few characters were lounging at the corner of an intersection twenty yards away, but they were the usual touts looking for handouts.

The barman looked at me as I went inside, didn't

recognise me as one of the regulars, and nodded in a friendly way. Most likely he had me tagged already—a guy who always got into trouble.

"Straight bourbon," I said, eyeing the joint. The place was almost empty, but there were one or two characters who'd obviously been there throughout the night.

The barman poured the drink, then settled his elbows on the bar and eyed me curiously.

"Been doing the town?" he inquired.

"Some," I agreed. "Why, anything happened?"

He polished a glass in an absent manner, then the leaned over the bar so that his face almost touched mine. "They say that Maxie Temple tried to make a comeback last night, only they got him at the airport. Only just stepped off the plane, so they say."

"Maxie Temple, eh?" I feigned surprise. "Have they got the guy who did it?"

"No. The cops couldn't pick anybody up even if they saw him do it with their own eyes." The barman sounded sarcastic.

"You got all this information from the police?"

He looked scared for a minute, licking his lips as he eyed me up and down.

"Just who are you?" he asked thinly.

"Don't worry about that," I said quickly. "I'm not from the police, if that's what you're worried about. It's just that I knew Maxie in the old days. We weren't exactly friends, but now that he's dead, I thought there might be something I could do to find his killer."

"Don't bother about that. Clancy Snow was around

here last night. Seems he's interested in that, too."

I kept quiet and finish my drink. Clancy Snow! It hadn't taken him long to get his teeth into the case. He wouldn't mention my name, of course. Everything would have to be done efficiently, and discreetly.

Do something, Johnny. Don't just sit there drinking bourbon and wait for them to close in on you. Maybe, even now, they're outside, cruising around in their lush limousines, eyes alert, scanning the early morning crowds, hoping to pick you out.

I got up, tossed a coin onto the polished top of the bar and hurried out. I would learn nothing there.

Twenty minutes later I was cruising through the slum quarter of Los Angeles, watching the bars and the people on the sidewalks. Somewhere, behind one of the hundreds of faces, in a quick and furtive brain, there would be the information I wanted. But how to find it?

It wasn't until an hour later that I spotted a face among the others that I recognised immediately. Square-jawed, with a thin, clipped moustache. The soft, brimmed hat was there, too, pulled low over the eyes, and it was that which first attracted my attention to him. I slowed the car to a crawl, following him at a respectable distance.

He gave no sign that he knew he was being followed, and a moment later disappeared down a small back alley. I stopped the car, got out, and went after him.

A door closed softly halfway down the alley. There was urgent tension building up inside me again, and I was suddenly glad of the .38 in my pocket. I slipped it out, checked it, then pushed open the door.

There was a hallway beyond and a half-open door at the end of it. Cautiously, I pushed it open, kicked it hard so that it slammed back against the wall, then went inside.

The hoodlum was coming for me fast and I tried to bring the gun up to cover him, even though I knew at the back of my mind that there wasn't time for that.

I was half-turned by the time he got to me, standing as a solid target for the straight right that he threw at my jaw. The blow knocked me against the table. He was lunging forward again, but I slid sideways to the right, going down onto the rough carpet as my feet caught up against a chair.

The gun was knocked spinning from my hand and clattered into a corner of the room, where it slid out of sight. So this was it. A fight to the finish with all the advantage of surprise on his side this time.

I swung the chair up as he turned, got it between us and lifted it towards his face. It blocked his headlong rush, but he pulled it savagely away from me before I could use it as a club to batter over his head.

His body twisted as he threw the chair across the room and I kicked out at him, sending him sprawling. He drew his lips back over his teeth in a grin of savage fury. His breath was whistling between his teeth as he tried to pull himself upright.

I lashed out at him again, but he rolled out of range, got to his feet with an agility that belied his bulk, and then he got to me with both fists pummelling my chest with rib-crushing blows that knocked all the wind from my body.

I doubled up, tried to get my breath back, and caught a savage blow on the chin that sent me reeling backwards, hitting the floor with my shoulders and spine. From the corner of my eye I caught a glimpse of the hoodlum's distorted features leaning over me as he drew back his foot to kick me in the small of the back.

I could see his face quite clearly, his teeth showing white in a tight grin of savage pleasure, his chest heaving beneath his torn coat. He looked down at me, then laughed harshly.

"I warned you last night I'd remember that beating, Merak," he gasped. "Now the boot's on the other foot and this is where you get what's coming to you."

He turned his attention away from me for a moment as he looked across to where the .38 had fallen, and it was that momentary mistake on his part that gave me the chance I needed.

Before he could move, I lashed out with my right foot, kicking him with all my strength on the ankle. With a yelled, he jumped backward and tripped over my other foot hooked behind his knee.

It wasn't easy to get up after the pummelling I had received earlier, but I managed it with a supreme effort. My head was spinning like a top and every breath seemed to rip my chest into a thousand pieces.

I knew inwardly that I had to move. Maybe the hoodlum would have killed me if I hadn't got the gun first. I don't know. He was almost on his feet when my fingers closed around it and I swung round, pointing it at his stomach.

"Just stay where you are, punk," I muttered, holding onto the table for support. "Otherwise I'll let you have it."

He stopped, glaring at me, his face twisting, his mouth working.

I knew the kind of man this hoodlum was. If he thought there was a chance in a million of taking back the gun from me, he'd have jumped at it. I could see by the glint in his eyes that if I let him go this time, no place on earth would be sufficiently distant for me to hide from him.

I wasn't really afraid, but it was a hell of a peculiar feeling.

"Sit down," I ordered. "There are a few questions I want to ask you."

He hesitated, then thought better of it, and sat down in one of the chairs. I moved around to where I could see him more clearly.

"It's obvious you knew I was following you, so it's pretty clear to me that you haven't let up on me."

"We never let up. You ought to know Clancy Snow better than that."

"Ah, so it's Clancy you're working for. I wondered about that, you know."

He looked sullen, stared down at the floor beneath his feet. I waited.

"So I'm working for Clancy Snow. What about it?"

"Nothing. Only perhaps you know more about what happened to Maxie Temple than I do. And I want to know something more. So if you want to get out of here in one piece, you'd better talk, otherwise I'll have the great pleasure of shooting you. It won't kill you outright, but you will linger long enough to suffer. Before the end, you'll be pleading with me to kill you."

The muscles on his face were working overtime now. I could see that he was getting scared and knew that it was no idle threat. His eyes kept flicking from my face to the gun in my hand and then back again.

"You can't scare me that easy," he said finally, licking his lips.

"No? Your yellowness is showing through your face." I steadied the gun and applied a little pressure on the trigger.

He leaned forward with a jerk and there were little beads of sweat popping out on his forehead. His hands gripping the size of the chair were white-knuckled with the nervous pressure he was exerting.

"Tell me what happened at the airport last night," I said gently. "All the details. Take your time. I can wait."

"You're a son of a bitch!" he spat sharply.

I brought the gun up just a shade. "Going to talk?" I asked.

He tried to nod his head and bleated a noise. My right elbow was ready to smash into his throat if he needed persuading.

"Clancy Snow arranged it, but you'll never prove

that. He's too smart for a crook like you to pin a murder rap on him."

"Who killed Maxie? Did you?"

He shook his head. "I wouldn't be that stupid. My job was to look after you, not Maxie."

"Then who did?"

"I don't know."

I hit him across the side of the face, jerking his head back viciously.

He glared with a naked fury at me, and for a moment I thought he intended to ignore the gun and make a lunge for me. Instead, he cooled off and sank back into the chair.

His voice took on a whining edge: "It's true, I tell you, I've no idea who did the killing. Do you think Clancy Snow would tell me that?"

Well, that was that. Once again I'd drawn a rotten break. I ought to have realised it, of course. Clancy Snow was a smart operator. He had plenty of men to carry out his orders. He didn't need to let any one of them know what the others were doing. And if they were smart, they didn't spill it either.

"Do you know anybody else at the airport, or did you see anybody who might have killed Maxie Temple?"

"Blast you, Merak! I've just told you, I don't know who rubbed him out."

"And I think you do."

He ran his tongue around his lips and made a little helpless gesture with his right hand.

"Clancy would kill me if he knew."

"And I'll kill you if you don't tell me," I warned him. "Remember that I've got the gun, not Clancy Snow."

"I realise that." He looked uncomfortable. "It could have been Alfred Madden. He was in the vicinity last night."

"Madden? I remember him. Dutch McKnight's muscleman. "So Dutch is in on it, too. I thought so."

"You'll never pin it on either of them, Merak."

"Never mind about that. Where can I get hold of Madden?"

He shook his head. "Nobody knows where Madden goes after he's finished the day job. Only Clancy Snow and Dutch. And you don't expect them to tell you, do you?" He laughed harshly.

"No, but if I remember correctly, Madden had a girlfriend, didn't he? I think I'll look her up. Maybe she'll be a little more cooperative than you." I backed towards the door, never taking my eyes off him for a moment. He was a rat and there was no telling when he would turn. He made his pitch just when I thought he would, dropping to his knees as I opened the door and then lunging forward, clawing for my legs.

He was still reaching forward, eyes wide and arms outstretched, when I pulled the trigger and felt the gun jerk against my wrist.

He collapsed forward onto his face as the bullet took him in the chest, fingers clawing at the carpet.

CHAPTER FOUR
BLACKIE SPORELLI

I opened the door, half-ran along the deserted length of the hallway, and got out—fast. There was a silencer on the .38, but there were still plenty of cops in that neighbourhood, who had the uncanny knack of being able to smell a murder a couple of blocks away.

A lot of sets of eyes turned and looked me over as I hurried from the alley, but there was little curiosity in their stare, and nobody made any move to stop me, so I guess they hadn't heard anything. Behind the wheel, I gunned the car and gave her everything she'd got and a lot more besides.

I didn't want to see Dawn, not just yet, anyway, so soon after killing a man. I didn't really understand anything about her, how she'd take the news, whether I ought to tell her or leave her in ignorance.

Stopping off again at Frenchie's, I parked the car ready for a quick take-off, just in case it should be necessary. Why, God knows. Because if Clancy Snow or any of the others got to know my immediate whereabouts, there wasn't a joint in Los Angeles with sufficient exits for me to get out.

I pushed open the door and went inside. The bar was crowded now, and there was the high-pitched laughter of women and the low harshness of men's conversation. Cigarette smoke with bitter in the air.

There seemed to be a rotten taste in my mouth like a ball of cotton wool, and I knew I needed a drink. This was the first time it began to get real dirty. Back in the old days with Maxie Temple, there had been hoodlums who'd been rubbed out when they got in the way. But somehow that had been different. The fellow back in that deserted house had never really had a chance once I'd got my hands on the gun. He was as good as dead before he'd got to his knees.

I thought about Dawn and wished she'd never got mixed up in this dirty business. It was no place for a woman. I'd spend most of the day and night fooling myself. Trying to convince myself they'd never get around to her. But it wasn't any use.

After the fifth drink I wasn't thinking too clearly. If I had to, I'd kill some more. But there didn't seem to be much sense to it.

I noticed the barman sizing me up with his eyes. He was still dubious, still curious. The trouble was, he might start adding two and two together and then the trouble would really start.

There were dozens of bars like this in the east side of Los Angeles, and the majority of them stayed open because they paid a handsome protection fee to Clancy Snow or Dutch McKnight. Those who didn't or who bucked against the idea were wrecked completely by a bunch of hoodlums, liquor smashed, furniture splintered into matchwood.

After that they either closed down shop or received a second ultimatum. Very few ignored that. It just wasn't healthy to defy the Organisation twice.

"You looking for somebody, friend?" The barman's eyes narrowed at me across the bar. I saw his teeth, big and yellow with nicotine under thin, bluish lips.

"Not really," I said. I wanted to know where Madden's girlfriend hung out, but I didn't intend to ask directly. Either he'd shut up like a clam or slip away at the first chance and phone Clancy Snow that a guy was asking too many leading questions and what was he to do with him.

"The hell with it," he muttered. "There's something on your mind. This is the second time you've been here in the past hour. And you look as though you have been through the mill. What's the beef, friend? Looking for trouble?"

He spoke through his teeth, lips drawn well back.

He was sizing me up with his eyes, not quite sure of me but determined to find out. I recognised his type at once, even with a mind blurred with alcohol. I wasn't that drunk. He was hand in glove with the Big Boys. Barroom brawls and street fights were a pleasure to such men. They thrived on it.

"Just downtown for a visit," I lied. "Nothing special."

He smiled, then stopped and just looked. He didn't believe me. "I got the idea you're asking too many questions. What's between you and this guy Maxie

Temple?"

"Maxie? I used to know him in the old days, just vaguely. He was one of the Big Shots. Everybody knew Maxie."

"He was a swell guy. Until he crossed up the Organisation and ran out on them. They didn't like that, you know. Nobody makes a fool of them and gets away with it."

He had both of his big, horn-nailed hands on the top of the bar now, looking straight at me. I knew now how to get what I wanted from him without arousing his suspicions.

All I had to do was treat him as one of the boys in the know, play dumb, and let him do all the talking, with only a bit of prompting now and again.

"Sure, I understand. But what about the others? Clancy Snow and Dutch and Alfred Madden. They're the Big Shots now, aren't they?"

The barman nodded his bulky head and picked up a bar rag. "They run things around here, if that's what you mean. Nobody knows much about McKnight. He's comparatively new around Los Angeles. Originally he came in from Detroit. Clancy Snow's been around ever since I can remember. He's in politics a little bit and handles real estate, but his real business is the protection racket and running illicit liquor."

"Sounds like a regular guy," I said. The tension was over.

The barman laughed, big and loud. "You might say he runs this part of town. We've got a D.A., but he's in

Snow's pocket. That's how he got elected and he takes what orders he's given."

The interesting thing to my way of thinking was how Snow and the others had managed to stay in power for as long as they had. Working on the outside of the racket as I had, one could sense the whirlpool in the centre. It would take a dammed good man to expose these men, bring them and their dirty activities out into the open, and give them a good airing.

They very seldom did the killings themselves, they had men to do them without asking questions. Men who could be trusted not to talk. I could feel the ruthless edge of fear and cruelty that was inherent in the Underworld Organisation, and I knew that it was this fear and cruelty that was their strength.

I had to find Madden. And to do that I needed to locate Cleo Newton, his girlfriend. Maybe if I could get hold of her, I'd be able to fight back. It was a hellish sensation, waiting there and feeling trapped and defeated. As the hoodlum had said: "Nobody knows where Madden goes after pulling off a job for the Big Men."

But Cleo Newton would know if anybody did.

If only I could get to her before the others did. They'd beaten me to Maxie Temple. Now, maybe, they'd figured out what I intended to do. They'd know I was standing around doing nothing.

I thought about that dead man lying stretched out on the blood-stained carpet in the house not more than half a mile away and wondered when the cops would get around to him.

When they did, Clancy Snow and his Highland would know about it in minutes, if they didn't find him first. And it wasn't like them to pass up on a deal like that. The finger of suspicion would point straight at Johnny Merak.

"Seen anything of Madden lately?" I asked. "Alfred Madden."

"Dutch McKnight's muscle-boy? No. He never comes around these parts unless he's got a job on hand." The barman shrugged and started to smile, then stopped as if he'd thought better of it.

His gaze had gone past me, to the door at my back. I didn't bother to turn my head: there was no need for that. Some kind of sixth sense, sharpened over the years, warned me that somebody had just come in, and as far as I was concerned, it wouldn't be a friend.

Someone crashed into the seat next to me. I glanced round, out of the corner of my eye. It wasn't a friend.

Blackie Sporelli. Whether that was his real name, nobody seemed to know. Mostly, you saw Blackie after dark, haunting the flashier nightspots of Balboa Bay or even as far afield as Beverly Hills. Slick and suave, he didn't look the professional killer, but he'd learned his business well in Detroit or Chicago or some other place. I knew Blackie Sporelli pretty well.

Short, dapper guy with black curly hair, well oiled and brushed so that it shone in the light. Clipped moustache, smart clothes, and hard eyes. Apart from his name, I knew his record; arrested three times for illegal possession of heroin and once on a charge of suspected murder. Then there had been talk about white slave traffic somewhere out East and his name had been mentioned in connection with it. But all of that was old stuff of a couple of years back.

Since he'd teamed up with Clancy he'd kept his nose clean and allowed his hired gunmen to do all the dirty work for him.

A changed guy? A solid, dependable citizen? I didn't think so, but it was surprising how many people did. The barman made to move away, picking up his rag, but Blackie called him back.

"Don't go away, buster. A couple of drinks for my friend here." A low, gentle voice and dark eyes watching me.

"Yes, Mr. Sporelli."

Blackie swung idly on his stool. He was smiling a little. A big cat, watching a little mouse squirm. Behind him stood a couple of thugs, hands in pockets, ready for me to make a dive.

"Hello, Johnny. Been looking for you all over, boy." No expression on his face. He knew that I'd only to make one wrong move and I'd pay for it. Not here, in the bar, but in some deserted backstreet outside, away from the crowds, where there would be nobody to witness the crippling, the going-over.

Most likely they'd bust my kidneys or break my ribs. The usual treatment for troublesome guys.

I looked him in the eye. "Looking for me, Blackie? Why?"

"We thought you might be in trouble. Now that Maxie's dead, the police seem to think you had something to do with it. Believe me, you're hot and no mistake."

"So I'm hot. Don't tell me that Clancy Snow is feeling generous and wants to help me?"

Blackie's features never altered under the insult, his eyes never wavered. The drinks came and he waited for me to take up mine before he lifted his own. Slowly, he turned the glass in his hands, the nails well manicured, the fingers delicately shaped, but strong.

"Drink up, Johnny," he said. "After all, we're old friends."

Like hell we are, I thought. But I didn't say it out loud. I wanted to keep my body in shape as long as possible. Instead, I downed the raw spirit, felt it down the back of my throat, then go down into my stomach where it exploded in an expanding cloud of warmth. Sporelli sipped his slowly.

"Just between the two of us," he said, leaning forward, "what did you expect to get from killing Maxie Temple?"

"You kidding?" I muttered. "You know damned well I didn't kill him. I wanted the chiseller alive and kicking. He was no good to me dead."

Sporelli smiled and replaced his glass on the bar. He would never understand why I wanted to finish with the whole rotten business, not even if I wrote it down for him, so I didn't bother to try.

"If you didn't kill him, you've got nothing to worry

about, have you, boy?" he said softly. "But Clancy seems to have other ideas and he'd like to straighten them out as soon as possible. He suggested you came with us, just for a talk, nothing more."

Still no threat in the quiet voice. But I knew Blackie Sporelli of old. He could discuss a guy's murder as dispassionately as he talked about the weather. I knew that once I stepped out of the door with them, I'd vanish off the face of the map until some guy, "dragging" the bed of the L.A. "river," pulled me from the surface of the concrete channel.

It was as simple as that. If I wanted to stay alive and in one piece, I would have to move fast.

"And what if I don't particularly want to see Snow just now?" I could see I'd asked the wrong question.

The steady gaze never wavered, but the full lips twitched back into a wide grin.

"Clancy wouldn't like that," he murmurs softly. He picked up his empty glass and held it up to the light, and as if it had been a signal, the two boys moved in with the precision of soldiers on parade. They were looking for trouble, ready for it, hoping I'd make some.

"You coming, Merak?"

I shrugged, but my brain was spinning like a dynamo in my head. The barman was several feet away at the other end of the bar, busily polishing a trayful of glasses. His whole attitude screamed loudly that he wanted no part in the quarrel.

There were two ways out of the bar. The front entrance and the back. I guessed they would take me out the back way. Less crowded, and there would be a car waiting with the driver already behind the wheel, the engine ticking over.

I got up slowly and wondered whether I'd ever get a chance to use the gun in my pocket. It wasn't likely, but I'd have a damned good try. I tried to think as I walked towards the rear exit, the two thugs ranged on either side of me, Sporelli bringing up the rear.

There was a narrow passage beyond the door. It looked deserted and the door at the far end was shut.

Maybe twenty seconds before they got me outside. Not long in which to save your life. I waited until one of the hoodlums reached out to open the door, then moved. Swinging, I hit the other under the ear with the heel of my left hand, knocking him against the tiled wall.

Sporelli started to shout even as I turned on him, grabbed the lapels of his jacket, pushed it down over his arms, and hit him in the stomach with my knee. He screamed twice, thinly, in writhing agony. It was the move I wanted. Before he could straighten, I turned him on his heel so that he now stood between me and the guy at the door, who was coming forward fast, his hand clawing for the gun in his pocket.

Luckily, the passage was narrow and Sporelli made a good shield. He was moaning softly to himself as I backed away with him. The second tough still slumped against the tiled wall, his head hanging drunkenly on his chest. He looked as though he had just been beaten to death.

"Kill him! Kill him!" Somehow Sporelli managed to find his voice and began to yell.

He wasn't so sure of himself any longer. Probably he could see himself answering to the Big Bosses for this stupid slip-up on his part. I couldn't envy him the job, but I still had to get away myself.

Hooking my foot around Sporelli's ankle, I shoved him forward, at the same time chopping him down with the edge of my hand behind his left ear. As he dropped, stumbling into the tough at the door, I turned and ran.

It was a busy mix-up while it lasted, which was about twenty seconds. Then I was diving along the passage, out through the crowded bar and into the street.

There was a black sedan parked against the kerb in front of Dawn's car. I didn't wait to give it a second glance. I backed the car, slid it up onto the kerb, spun the wheel, and gunned it out into the middle of the traffic. A heavy truck passed within inches, the driver leaning out of his cab and yelling something unintelligible, as I passed into the westbound lane. I watched Frenchie's joint in the rear mirror until it was out of sight.

The black sedan hadn't moved from its position against the kerb. Maybe I'd tagged the wrong guy. Maybe he was just another ordinary fellow who happened to be there at that moment.

The bitterness and the tension inside me were beginning to rankle again. Too much was happening, too fast. I could feel the wheels of the Organisation beginning to turn, the net beginning to close. The pick-up order had already gone out from the gang bosses. "Get Johnny Merak, dead or alive!"

Perhaps the police had put out one, too. Whether they had or not, I was still in one hell of a fix.

I twisted in and out of the traffic for almost an hour, just in case they'd had put a tail on me. Whatever happened, I didn't want to lead them back to Dawn.

I knew what would happen once they got their claws into her. My own face didn't look any too good. A couple of bruises under one eye and a lump inside my lip where a tooth had pushed into it that felt like a piece of cotton-wool, permanently fixed into place.

Down below my chest ached and there was a dull nausea in the pit of my stomach. But I had to drive that car so that they wouldn't follow me and I had to stay in Los Angeles until this business was finished for good, one way or another. Even though I felt as though all I wanted was to crawl away somewhere and sleep for a week.

I stopped the car outside a phone booth and called Dawn's number. I figured that was safer than going straight there, just in case they were smarter than I thought and already had her cased.

"Hello?" Even over the phone her voice sounded low and husky and did things to me that no other woman's had ever done before.

"That you, Dawn?" I asked. I knew it was, but I wanted to play it safe.

"Johnny!" She said the single word as though she

hadn't expected to hear from me ever again.

I threw a swift glance through the glass panelling of the booth.

"Where are you speaking from, Johnny?"

"A phone booth downtown. Listen carefully, Dawn. They may have a tail on me, but I don't think so. How's everything out there? Anybody suspicious nosing around? Phoney gas-repairmen or anything like that?"

"No. Nothing like that, Johnny."

"Good. Then maybe there's still a chance. Can you meet me somewhere? It's important. I need help and I think you may be able to steer me onto the right track."

"All right, Johnny. I'll meet you on the corner of Seventh and Twelfth in ten minutes."

"I'll be there," I said, and hung up.

I didn't like to bring her into it, but I was in a spot where I had to clutch at anything. It's usually difficult to protect a woman, any woman, at the price of your own skin. Some guys might be able to do it. Maybe even Johnny Merak. But I figured he'd be kind of lonely if he did.

CHAPTER FIVE
A DATE WITH CLEO

Dawn was standing on the corner of Seventh and Twelfth looking a little lost and uncertain. She spotted me almost at once and I swung the car into the side, opening the door for her. Her delicate features went tight for an instant as she slipped in beside me, her eyes searching mine, taking in the bruises and the cut on my face.

"Something's happened, Johnny. Trouble?"

"In a way, yes. I ran into Blackie Sporelli and a couple of his strong-arm boys downtown. I wasn't looking for trouble, seems I just attract it."

She turned to look at me as we headed off into the streaming traffic again. She was waiting for me to go on.

"I've got to get hold of a man called Alfred Madden. It's important. He's in town somewhere, but nobody seems to know where he goes after finishing a job for the Big Men."

"Finishing a job?"

"That's right. I have an idea it was Madden who shot Maxie Temple last night. He fits the bill and I happen to know he was around at the airport when it happened."

Dawn gasped. I felt her body stiffen against mine and her features hung a little slack. There was a look on her face as if all hope had died mourning inside her. Her hands tightened on her lap.

"And you intend to kill him, Johnny?"

I shrugged. "I don't know. It depends on whether he decides to talk. I've no quarrel with him simply because he killed Maxie Temple. I'd have done the same myself once I'd got what I wanted from him."

"How can I help you to find this man?"

"You can't. First I'll have to get hold of his girl-friend. She's the only one outside of Clancy Snow and the other Big Men who might know where he's lying low."

"What's her name?" asked Dawn. Her voice was suddenly flat and emotionless.

"Cleo Newton," I said, feeling like a heel. "Ever heard of her?"

"Yes."

We both let it go at that for a long moment, while I concentrated on driving, watching her occasionally out of the corner of my eye. She was fighting within herself. I could see that. I cut into one of the quieter streets, away from the mainstream of traffic.

Her eyes searched my face, then she said: "I said last night I'd help you all I could, Johnny. I meant that, but I don't want to see you get yourself killed."

"I'll try not to, Dawn," I said. "But if I don't stop these people, somebody else will step off the plane at the airport or the bus terminus and walk into a bullet. Can't you see that?"

She smiled bitterly. "I sat alone in my room this morning after you'd gone. There was a lot I had to think about, such a lot. But I was alone with it and it was all inside me, so I couldn't run away from it and I had to face up to it. Maybe it sounds selfish, but I wanted you alive, not lying on some slab in the city mortuary."

"This is straight. You're right. But I've got to go through with it. If you don't help me, I'll have to find somebody else who can."

Dawn looked away, her lips tight. I thought I saw the glint of tears in her eyes, but if there were, she blinked them away and they were quite dry when she looked at me again.

"All right, Johnny. I hope you know what you're doing. I used to know Cleo Newton a year or so ago. She had a flat on the outskirts of town. I can't guarantee that she still there, but I'll show you the place if it'll help you."

"Thanks," I said, and I really meant it.

Only when we reached the blare and noise of the outskirts did I realise how little chance I would have had of finding Cleo Newton by myself. The midday traffic in the suburbs was heavier than I had expected, heavy trucks running into the industrial areas, businessmen hopping to snatch a short hour at home or in the restaurants during their lunchtime break.

Dawn lit a cigarette. I didn't say anything to break the silence, even though I knew she was waiting desperately for words to comfort her, convince her she was doing the right thing. But whatever tumult was storming away inside her mind, she didn't allow it to show in her face.

We rounded a long curve that was a teeming mass of cars and trucks.

"How bad is it really, Johnny?" she asked, breaking the silence.

I answered her slowly. "It's really bad if this break doesn't pan out. Whatever I've got coming to me, I'll have to take. As soon as a man steps out of line and defies the Underworld bosses, he becomes a menace and has to be removed. I guess I'm such a menace."

"Why don't you give yourself up to the police, Johnny? Have they got anything on you?"

"Only the murder of Maxie Temple and a couple of hoodlums. Nothing that can't send me up for the big burn," I said bitterly.

"But why? Johnny? Why? Why? Why?" She spread her hands. "How did it all start in the first place?"

"*Start?* How does it ever start? Maybe I was plain stupid getting into the racket in the first place. The Big Men are clever. You begin by collecting debts from the downtown bookies, and before you know where you are, the bug's bitten you."

"But why don't you get out before it can taint you with its filth?"

"It's too late then, Dawn. You have been careless. Forged cheques, petty larceny, perjury, things like that. They have it all down in black and white with your name scrawled across the bottom. They put the collar on you deliberately."

"Is it always as bad as that?"

"Worse. Every now and then something would crop up that really stank. Putting the finger on some prominent businessman or politician so that a crooked guy, backed by Maxie Temple, got elected. Do you wonder I've so few friends?"

It was a little after eleven when we reached the suburban district of Los Angeles. Here the houses are all the same, tired and dingy-looking. Perhaps they'd been fresh some thirty years before. Here and there somebody had a little garden in front of their house, but even the flowers looked faded and dead, as though they had given up trying.

I moved the car slowly along the kerb as Dawn peered at the tiny metal numbers on the green-painted doors.

"That's it," she said finally, pointing.

I stopped the car. Cleo Newton's house was a dingy affair like the rest in the street. There was a woman washing the steps in front of it.

"Does a Miss Newton live here?" asked Dawn.

The woman looked up, wiping her hands on her apron. She looked old, but she wasn't really. No more than thirty-six, I figured, but the years had left their mark on her features. She had been pretty once, but not now.

"Cleo Newton?" She looked surprised.

"Yes. Cleo Newton," I said.

She climbed stiffly to her feet. "Sure, she lives here."

"Is she in?"

The woman thought about that for a minute. I dug down into my pocket and brought out a five-dollar bill. Her head turned briefly and I saw greed in her eyes.

She nodded quickly, nervously, her eyes bright like a bird's. "I'll tell her but I don't think she'll see you. She doesn't see many people, not lately, anyway."

"Don't bother to do that," I interrupted quickly. "Just tell us her room number and we'll go up."

"I don't know whether I ought to—"

"It's all right," said Dawn. "She's a friend of mine. She won't mind."

"Well—if you're sure." She looked up at me help-lessly, then nodded. "Room Five. It's on the first floor."

She took the bill eagerly, watched us as we climbed the steps, then went on with her washing again.

It was good to be so near to something at last. I walked with slow, deliberate steps, although my ribs ached abominably, and there was a sharp, agonising pain striking from the muscles of my right leg with every step. But now that I was on the right track again, I forgot all my aches and pains and followed Dawn up the narrow, winding stairs. There was a sharp smell of dust in the air that caught at my nostrils.

We found the room at the top of the stairway, the number hanging askew on the door. Dawn knocked softly. We waited then, when there was no reply, knocked louder.

Still no sound from the other side of the door. I

looked across at Dawn. "Doesn't look as though she's home."

"But the housekeeper was sure she was in. You'd have thought she'd have known if Cleo had gone out."

"Yeah," I said. I began to feel that empty way inside. I tried the door. It was open.

We went in together. I thought I knew what to expect. The room empty. Cleo gone and with her my last hope. But it wasn't like that at all.

Cleo Newton was there all right, lying in a wide chair in front of the empty hearth. Dawn gave a little scream that died in her throat and clutched my arm.

"Is she—is she dead?"

"I don't know." I started for her, felt for her pulse. It was still beating strongly, but irregularly. There was a hypodermic on the carpet, lying where it had fallen from her nerveless fingers.

I picked it up. There was still something in it, a clear liquid I couldn't identify. But the expression on her face was enough to tell part of the morbid story. Her body was light, easy to pick up and place carefully on the bed. I pulled one of the cushions from the chair and slipped it beneath her head.

"What is it, Johnny?" There was concern in Dawn's voice as she knelt beside the bed.

"This," I said, holding out the hypodermic. "Just the kind of senseless, rotten break I expected. I knew it was too good to last. But why, why, why?" I could almost feel the hands of my watch grinding the way around the circular face. "She's a dope addict," I said bitterly. "Heroin, by the look of it. No wonder they didn't think she was worth bothering about. Why they didn't decide to silence her for good. She's too far gone to remember anything."

"Poor Cleo," said Dawn. "She was a fine kid once. I'm sorry I saw her like this. I'd have preferred to remember her as she was. Laughing and kind, without a care in the world. What makes people do these kind of things?"

"Who knows?" I said harshly. "Why do any of us do these things?"

"What shall we do with her, Johnny?"

"There's nothing we can do. Nobody can help her now. She's too far gone. Leave her where she is. She'll come out of it soon and remain sane for perhaps a couple of days until she gets her hands on another shot."

"But we can't just leave her like this."

"Sure we can. She's a lush and nothing is going to change that." I walked away towards the door, feeling sour and bitter inside.

Dawn paused for an instant beside the bed, then reached a decision and followed me. Outside in the corridor, she caught my arm tightly. "You're rotten in places," she said. "So ruthless and empty. God, you must be completely soulless. But there's something about you, Johnny, that I can't get out of my mind."

CHAPTER SIX
INTRODUCING CLANCY SNOW

It was the big fix. Indirectly, of course. This drug addiction of Cleo Newton's hadn't been a sudden thing, raised on the spur of the moment. It had been coming for months, perhaps years, building up like a time bomb inside her. Probably they'd given her the stuff in the first place, just in case anybody got around to tying her up with Madden and started asking awkward questions.

I began to feel finished. First Maxie Temple—and now this. The chips were being stacked against me so solidly that I couldn't move.

Inside the car we didn't talk much. I could see that Dawn had been shocked by what she has seen. Now, for perhaps the first time, it was coming home to her what these people were like I was fighting. I could see she hadn't believed it at first. It was like some bad dream. Something that happened to the other guy, but never to yourself.

"I still don't understand why Cleo should do such a thing as that." There was a mute inquiry in Dawn's voice. "She had everything when I knew her. Not too much money, but enough. She didn't have to get mixed up in this dirty business. She was clean and decent."

"Most of us start off that way, Dawn," I said helplessly. "It's when we try to stay like it that the fun starts. Maybe she got a rotten break somewhere along the line."

I shut up then. It had happened to me, but not in quite the same way. I'd gone into it with my eyes open. Cleo Newton might have been different. It was easy the way the peddlers did it. A cigarette that didn't look any different from the ordinary kind, only this one contained that little bit extra—marijuana.

Maybe that one cigarette would have cost the peddler a couple of dollars, maybe more. But it was worth it. After the first draw, the craving would start, building up insidiously, gradually, until it had such a hold on the victim that they couldn't break loose.

Then the big money would start to roll in. Not a handful of bucks, but thousands. And if they couldn't pay, they are either died, or were taken off to some institution where they underwent the torturous treatment that never really worked.

Somewhere along the line, Cleo Newton had fallen into the web, and now all that was left of her was that empty shell lying back there in a dingy room where the sun scarcely ever shone and everything reeked of squalor and stale liquor.

The street in front of Dawn's place was empty, and a glance in the rear mirror showed me that we weren't being followed. I parked the car and we both got out.

Dawn opened the door with her key and I followed her inside.

Pushing open the door of the inner room, I had time to see the tall figure in the chair before a well-known voice said:

"I thought I'd find you here somehow, Johnny. Come inside. And bring the lady in, too, I don't like to be kept waiting."

Clancy Snow. The Big Shot. And funnily enough, he was all alone.

Dawn came in and stood beside me. There was no fear on her face such as I could feel boiling around in my stomach. For a long time I'd tried to keep out of the way of men such as Snow and McKnight. But if they wanted trouble, they'd get it.

I walked forward, putting on a bold front, hoping I didn't look as scared as I felt inside.

Clancy Snow. Tall and thin with a mane of prematurely white hair that matched his name. Pale blue eyes, like chips of ice, cold and ruthless.

Well-cut clothes, an expensive ring on the second finger of his right hand that flashed whenever he moved his arm, a fixed kind of smile frozen permanently on his face.

"You're a fool, Merak," he said softly, shaking his head. "Some very important people are interested in you. Very interested. And you know what a thing like that means to the Organisation."

"Yeah, I know." I tried to think why he'd come here and, above all, how he'd managed to locate me so fast.

Clancy Snow coming to talk to me in person and unattended by his usual retinue of stocky, strong-arm boys, could mean only one thing.

Johnny Merak was becoming more of a menace to them by the minute. I could almost see his cunning brain at work behind that smooth, suave exterior. He wasn't sure whether he had me figured right, and even if he had, what it all added up to.

His mind was busy asking questions and adding up every little detail. How had Sporelli slipped up and allowed me to escape from the trap? What was the next move going to be on my part? Was I still a danger to them and if so, how dangerous?

Those were the important questions as far as he was concerned, and he had to get the answers for himself. I knew he'd noticed the bruises and the cuts the minute I'd entered the room.

"Why don't you be reasonable, Johnny?" He was smiling frostily. "We don't want to make trouble with you. If you killed Maxie Temple, the agency can fix things for you, get you out of town for a spell until everything blows over. Fix you up at some quiet little place on the coast, maybe even arrange for your girlfriend to go with you."

Some nice, quiet little place. That was funny. What he really meant was he'd arrange for us to be picked up and taken to some deserted spot, quietly disposed of, and dumped in the ocean with a weight around our feet.

"I think I'll stick around, Clancy," I said, and it was

like spitting in his face.

"I'm sorry you feel that way." He spoke in a dreamy fashion as though taking little notice of anything I said. As if it didn't really matter, but he only wanted to keep up the conversation.

But that wasn't it all. There was some kind of photographic arrangement in his brain that was busy shuffling my answers back and forth, probing them, dissecting every word, every inflexion, assessing me.

He turned his pale-eyed gaze on Dawn, appraising her, not as a woman, but as something to be used against me should the necessity ever arise.

"You've changed, Johnny. What is it? You never used to talk this way, even after Maxie framed you and sent you up the river."

"Sure, I've changed," I said. I grimaced and sat down, facing him. "I'll do my best to put you in the picture. It isn't nice, but I guess you aren't used to decent things, so it won't shock you. Since I started with the Organisation I've done everything that's slimy and dirty and underhanded. I've been the big fix. Anything rotten that has to be done, anybody you wanted framed so that a decent guy gets slung out of office on his neck and one of the Organisation's candidates get selected, send for Johnny Merak. He'll fix it. The best little fixer in the business."

"You were well paid for anything you did," said Clancy, placing the tips of his fingers together.

"Sure, I got plenty of dough. And you saw to it that I made enough mistakes to keep me from ever getting out of line. Perjury and corruption with all the forged cheques put away carefully in your safe. Well, I'm sick of it all, the job, fixing politicians, everything."

"That could be a bad mistake on your part, Johnny. You know our methods. You've carried them out yourself often enough to be thoroughly familiar with them. I wouldn't want to see the lady's looks impaired in anyway, believe me, but—"

"You lay one finger on her, Snow, and I'll kill you. I know your methods and I'll be watching for them."

He laughed uneasily and got up. A tall, slim guy with a baby face and an expression that looked as though he couldn't harm a fly.

"I had hoped you'd see sense, Merak," he said, speaking softly. "Apparently I was mistaken. You've made yourself into a nuisance. Needless to say, we cannot tolerate this interference in our work. Effective at once, you no longer enjoy the protection of the Organisation."

He walked back to the door without once looking back. A moment later the front door closed and from the window I saw him walking towards the kerb. A powerful sedan appeared like magic from nowhere, picked him up, and vanished down the street.

Dawn was sitting in one of the chairs, her features straight and fixed. She was twisting a thin scarf between her fingers.

"I'll get some coffee," she said when she saw me watching her. "Has he gone?"

"Yes. He had a car waiting somewhere out of sight.

They'd have been within earshot if I'd started anything. Clancy Snow isn't a fool."

"How much more of this hell are you going to raise before you're finished, Johnny?" she asked, turning as she reached the door to the kitchen. Her voice sounded thick and tired.

"Just as much as is necessary," I said. "They're scared a little, afraid of how much I know."

"I'm scared, too. I didn't think I would be this morning, but I am. I went into this with my eyes open, and I mean to go through with it. But I'm still frightened."

We drank the coffee in silence. There was a lot I had to think about. Things were happening fast and the net was drawing tighter around me every minute. I wanted to get out and walk away, leave everything, especially Dawn, because as long as she tagged onto me, her life wasn't worth a bent nickel.

Clancy Snow would go back to his hideout and give the necessary orders to pull me in. If Dawn was lucky, she'd get off with a beating-up. If she wasn't, there were worse things they could do.

The sky was darkening outside and it looked like rain. I went over to the window, twitched the lace curtains back a couple of inches and looked out. They hadn't been long. A sleek Mercury stood parked on the opposite side of the street.

The driver was seated behind the wheel smoking a cigarette. There was another guy just getting out of the back. He went round and started talking to the fellow in the front. Further along the street two more were idling their time on the corner, and I didn't need to go around to the back to prove to myself that there were others watching that exit. They had me holed up like a rat with no place to turn.

My lighter flamed and I lit a cigarette. Dawn came over and stood beside me, close, so that I could feel the warmth of her.

"Give me a cigarette, Johnny," she said. I lit one for her and motioned towards the Mercury.

"They weren't long in getting on my tail," I remarked dryly. "Four of them out there already and I'll bet anything there are another half-dozen out at the back."

"Clancy Snow's men?"

"Right, first time."

"What do you intend to do now? You can't go out there. They'd shoot you down the first wrong move you made."

"I doubt it. They do want to take me alive if they could."

"Do you think they'll come up here?"

I shook my head. "They'll wait for a while, perhaps until it gets dark, before they try anything like that. This is a pretty respectable neighbourhood, compared to what they're used to. They won't want to make any fuss. Not if they can get me any other way."

"Is this the end, then?" A dispirited voice asking questions I couldn't answer.

It wasn't the end, really, I decided. For me it was just beginning all over again. I knew now what I was up against. I'd seen it happen too many times before, only then I'd been on the giving end. Now I was a sucker who was receiving the full treatment.

"There's only one thing left for me to do," I said. I hoped she couldn't see the defeated look in my face. "Maybe I should have thought of it before, but so many things were happening, it must have slipped my mind."

"What's that?"

"Those papers I want. Now that Maxie's dead, somebody must have them. Clancy Snow wasn't kidding when he threatened to finish me. It could be a one-way ticket into San Quentin that he's counting on. And the only way he can do that is to stick me with those charges that Maxie Temple was holding over me."

"You think this man Snow's got the papers?"

"It figures, doesn't it? The only other guy big enough is Dutch McKnight, and he hasn't made a move so far, so I'm banking on Clancy."

"Yes, it's all right knowing who's got them, but how are you going to get hold of them?"

"It's going to be tricky, but there's a way. I seem to remember Clancy having a hideout somewhere along Balboa Beach. If I could only get out there and slide past the thugs in the street, and if Clancy still had the same hideout after all these years, and if he was fool enough to keep papers like that hanging around in a safe I could open, I might still stand a chance of clearing myself and breaking him."

Looking at it that way, it looked promising, but everything seemed so dependent on a multitude of 'if's.

"Supposing they stop you? What then?"

"That's all in the luck of the draw. But one thing is clear. I can't stay here doing nothing, wondering what's going on out there, waiting for them to close in and finish me off."

"I understand, Johnny." She made it sound as though she really did, but there was doubt on her face.

"I'm trying to play it smart the first time in my life," I said, more to convince myself than her. "It isn't going to be easy. I think I'd better get some sleep if I can."

"Sure. I'll make up a place for you."

It took ten minutes to fall asleep. My face was still sore, although the dull ache in my ribs was beginning to go away. Instinctively, I took the .38 from my pocket and slipped it under the pillow, within easy reach. It was a purely reflex action.

It was nearly dark when I woke up, my chest stiff and cold. Pain shot through me as I moved and there was a taste in my mouth like fur. I pulled myself up, looked around for Dawn, but she wasn't there.

That brought me round with a jerk. I went through into the kitchen, figuring maybe she was fixing something to eat, but the place was deserted. It must have been five minutes later when I heard the front door click open, then close.

One idea cut through the fuzziness in my brain. While I'd slept they'd taken Dawn away and now they were coming back for me. The .38 was in my fist before the door to the room opened. I had it trained on whoever came in, although they seemed to be making plenty of noise about it.

Dawn came in with a pile of packages in her arms. She looked as though she had been running. I put the gun away and felt like a fool.

"I just slipped out for something to eat," she said, placing the packages on the table.

Somehow, I felt more mad than relieved. "Don't you know that was a dammed fool thing to do," I said. "Those hoodlums out there—do you think they're hanging around the place just for fun? You're damned lucky to have got back alive."

Why they hadn't picked her up, I couldn't figure. It wasn't like them to pass up a chance like that. The snatch was simple. A sedan moving slowly along the kerb. Nobody in sight, a quick grab, a push and the car was on its way again with the victim inside.

I didn't say much more after that. I think she realised what could have happened to her. I hung around at the window while she cooked the food she'd brought. The smell of it coming in from the kitchen reminded me how hungry I really was. Only one good meal that day and that had been first thing in the morning. A man can't do too much without good food inside and I had plenty to do.

I began to think about that place out at Balboa Beach, and I didn't relish the idea of going in there alone, but it was something which had to be done.

Dawn came in with a thick steak, and although the muscles of my face still hurt abominably as I chewed, it was well worth the effort. I followed it with black coffee and then a double Scotch. After that, I began to feel better. The fuzziness in my head began to fade and I could think properly.

By the time it was really dark, I was ready. Dawn's car was still parked outside, but they could be watching that like hawks, and it wasn't worth the risk. I clipped the .38, slipped it into my pocket after loading the spent chambers.

That night, unless I missed my guess, there was likely to be trouble. Better to be ready and meet it halfway than to blunder into it with my eyes shut.

I went to the door, opened it an inch, and peered out. The two hoodlums in the car were still there, watching the house. I couldn't see the others who'd been further along the street, but no doubt they were still there, somewhere. They didn't give up that easily.

"I'll slip out the back way," I said in a whisper. "There's more cover there. Better switch off the lights until I'm gone."

"Good luck." There was a kind of sob in Dawn's voice. She clung tightly to me for an instant, then broke away. "I don't know why I let myself feel like this about you, Johnny Merak," she said softly and I thought she was crying. "You're poison as far as I'm concerned, but darn it, I can't help myself."

"I'll be back, Dawn," I said. "I promise."

She switched off the lights and I opened the rear door and slipped out into the night.

CHAPTER SEVEN
BALBOA BEACH

The back of the building, unlike the front, was no fancy place. In the darkness, I banged my shins against upjutting stone walls that seemed to push themselves out of the blackness at my feet with an unceasing regularity.

All the time I tried not to think of the thugs who were undoubtedly waiting to pick me up the minute I showed my face.

I ran my fingers all the way along a wall, guided myself by it until I reached the iron grille gate that led out onto the street. There was a lamp less than ten yards away, and a tall, mean-looking character lounging under it.

No sense in going that way unless I wanted a fight. I felt my way around the wall until I reached the end of it, jumped for the top, holding my breath as my fingers started to slip, then wriggled myself over. My feet didn't make a sound when they hit the sidewalk, and I was away and into the shadows before the bright boy under the lamp thought of looking.

After that it was comparatively easy. I reached the

bright lights, saw that it was nearly ten-fifteen, and wondered how I was going to get out to Balboa Beach at that time of night.

I made my way down to the central bus terminus, found I had fifteen minutes to wait before the next one for Balboa and Newport Beach, and hung around, trying to stay in the background, inconspicuous.

Inside the bus it was cool, with a fresh breeze blowing through the half-open windows. There weren't many passengers. It was the last run. Most of the late-night crowds of the Los Angeles bars either stayed out all night, or had their own cars.

I wasn't all that good at cracking safes, especially the kind Clancy Snow would have in his secret hideout. But I thought I knew where I could pick up a good cracksman and one who wasn't all that scared of the Big Bosses either.

Mentally, I crossed my fingers. This was my last throw; if it didn't come off, I was as good as dead. It wasn't difficult to locate the cracksman. Mike Spangler spent ninety percent of his waking life in the Yellow Angel on Newport Beach.

Even though it was almost eleven-thirty, he was there as usual, seated on one of the round stools, half-swung round, looking at the world through the bottom of a glass. He nodded as he saw me, waved, not surprised.

"Hello, Johnny. Have a drink."

We might just have parted the evening before.

I sat down on the vacant stool next to him and lowered my voice. He didn't seem to be in too bad a shape and if he hadn't lost his touch since I had last seen him, he'd have that safe open in next to no time.

"I need your help, Mike," I said. "It's important and it's dangerous. If you come out with your skin intact, you'll be damned lucky."

Mike grinned. A little man with a wizened expression who'd seen the insides of as many prisons as he had safes.

I relaxed and drank the beer the barman placed in front of me. Its cool, catnip flavour tingled at the back of my throat, smoothed away some of the tension that had been building up inside me all day.

"For a pal like you, Johnny, I'll do anything. Just name the place. You don't need to ask my price, I'm only too pleased to help out."

I leaned forward more comfortably. "Ever been inside Clancy Snow's hideout, Mike?"

Mike's tiny eyes dug little holes to me. For once he seemed at a loss for words, then he whispered hoarsely: "Clancy Snow! You ain't thinking of breaking that safe, are you?"

"Think you could do it?"

"Are you kidding? It ain't the safe that worries me, I could crack that with my eyes shut. But—Clancy Snow! If we're caught in there, it's the end of the line for us. I suppose you know that."

"I know it," I said. "But I'm in a spot. There's nothing else I can do. And I need a good cracksman. You're the best in the business. What do you say?"

Mike screwed up his face. It was almost as though a

hand grenade had exploded in his brain, sending little sparks flashing into his eyes. I can understand what he was thinking about. The thought was a challenge to him.

He was master at his craft, an artist. A special breed of man. Maybe a mixture of Irish, Italian, and German all blended together about two generations back. A big-hearted guy who couldn't resist a safe, anxious to put his knowledge and skill against the guys who kept turning them out, claiming them to be foolproof, thief-proof, and everything else.

If he could break Clancy Snow's safe, it would be a feather in his cap, if he ever lived to tell the tale. Mike and I looked at each other. He let his breath out in a long sigh.

"Okay, Johnny. I'm with you. When do we pull it off?"

"Tonight," I said. "There isn't much time left. Think you can find your way out to Clancy's place?"

"Sure." He finished the rest of his glass. "But as you said before, it ain't going to be easy."

We walked out of the bar together. I didn't bother to turn my head, but I knew there were plenty of people looking at us. They would have recognised Mike, of course. My only chance of staying alive now was that they hadn't recognised me. If they had, there would be a reception committee waiting for us at the hideout.

The breeze blowing off the Pacific smelt of salt and there were wisps of spray in it that stung our faces. This was Newport, and it was a little difficult to realise that we were now almost forty miles south of Los Angeles.

It was a mixed town. Here the sportsman came during the summer and fall to play the marlin in the sweeping seas. Here the tourists came from the cities to relax and forget everything during a brief stay.

But it was here also that men came to get away from the Underworld and the Organisation. Men like Mike Spangler, who wanted to be forgotten, to be overlooked. Maybe if I'd come here at the beginning, I wouldn't be where I was now, rushing into something that could perhaps lead to my death.

Mike had his car outside at the kerb. A Mercury of ancient vintage. He slipped in behind the wheel and I climbed in beside him. There was still plenty of power in the car in spite of her appearance, and in less than ten minutes we were approaching the beach house, perched on a knoll of ground, well away from the others.

We parked the car well away from the house, went forward on foot. Our feet made no noise in the sand, and the .38 was a comforting bulge in my pocket.

"Can't see anybody about," whispered Mike. "Think it's safe to go in?"

I looked round. The sand dunes stretched away as far as the line of foam that marked the beginning of the Pacific. Nothing moved and the entire house in front of us was in darkness.

"Work your way around to the garage," I mumbled. "We should be able to tell from the number of cars they have got here. Clancy Snow was still in Los Angeles this afternoon. It's unlikely he'll come back here. Not tonight, anyway."

"I hope to God you're right." A low whisper close to my ear.

"He won't be expecting me here," I whispered back. "As far as he's concerned, I am still in that house with Dawn Grahame. He had a handful of thugs ringing it round."

"God. They must want you pretty bad, Johnny."

"Oh, sure," I said, sarcastically.

"You've got rocks in your head."

Rightly so. I'd been a proud guy once, able to think clearly, not caring what anyone thought or said about me. But all that was a long time before. I'd learn to despise the men and women in the rackets. The scheming women and the lying, cheating men, swarming around you with a smile when they need you; but when they didn't, you really saw their true nature. Cruel and utterly arrogant.

I took the gun out, hefted it into my right hand, and followed the thin figure of Mike Spangler towards a house that seemed to have a waiting quality hanging over it. I felt uneasy. A man can force himself to do things up to a certain point. Beyond that, he needs something more than mere courage. He needs hate.

And I hated Clancy Snow and Dutch McKnight and the whole rotten set-up.

Mike fiddled with the lock on the door for a couple of minutes, then opened it quietly.

There hadn't been any cars in the garage at the side

of the house and that made me feel a lot easier. If any of the thugs returned while we were still there, we would at least hear the sound of their car.

Where to now? I wondered. A good question. We were inside what amounted to the headquarters of the Underworld in Los Angeles. There was a dark entrance and a door at the end, which Mike opened cautiously.

I flashed the shaded torch around the place. Clancy Snow certainly did himself proud. I whistled quietly to myself as the beam flashed over the paintings on the wall. Some of them must have been worth plenty.

But they were the last things I saw. What I was really looking for was Clancy Snow's personal safe, and he wouldn't have that lying around for any cheap crook to walk in and rifle.

It wasn't easy to locate. By myself, I doubt whether I could have done it. But Mike seemed to have an uncanny knack of smelling out a safe a mile away.

In the next minute or two he'd find out how to crack it, his sensitive fingers easing the combination lock round a fraction at a time, listening for the tumblers to drop.

"It's not going to be easy," said Mike in a harsh whisper.

I wasn't really surprised. There were some pretty important papers in that safe, unless I was mistaken. Papers I wanted and intended to have.

There was a taut, insistent silence in the house.

Around us there was the wind-whipped darkness, the beach, the rolling surf, and the net drawing tighter around the neck of Johnny Merak.

CHAPTER EIGHT
GETAWAY

It was good to watch Mike at work. In the old days he had been a good man with safes, and it was plain to see that the intervening years had not dulled his perceptions in the least.

His fingers moved with quick but gentle motions, barely brushing the combination lock. My watch showed one-fifteen. I kept the beam of the torch as steady as possible, wishing that Mike would hurry up, get the safe open, so that we could pull out before anything happened.

I wondered what Dawn was doing. I hoped to God that she was still all right and that the thugs hadn't moved in, found me missing, and put two and two together. I could visualise Clancy Snow and his henchmen racing from Los Angeles in their Cadillacs, foaming at the mouth at the way I had beaten them to the punch.

Another long wait and at the end of it Mike seemed no nearer opening the safe than he had at the beginning.

"This is a new make," he said apologetically, wiping the sweat from his brow with the back of his sleeve.

"They must have learned something since I cracked my last."

"Stick to it, Mike," I urged. "Those papers—"

"If they're worth your neck, they must be important."

"If I can lay my hands on them, I'll be able to slash Clancy Snow and his rotten bunch of crooks for good."

"Good for you, Johnny." He turned back to his task, patient and unflagging.

In thirty-five minutes he had it open. A deep cavity in the wall, lined with papers that looked official and were really dynamite.

"Found anything?" asked Mike. He held the torch while I rifled through the papers.

Only when I'd read through the first half-dozen or so did I realise the full significance of them. Clancy Snow was something of a jack-of-all-trades as far as the rackets were concerned.

I knew just a little of what I was fighting. Illicit liquor deals. A vast rake-off from their racing tracks; underhand deals involving several million dollars a year. Contacts with a dozen television networks. A finger in everything that was dirty.

Clancy Snow, The Big Man, running an empire that stretched beyond Los Angeles and Newport Beach. The evidence here among these papers was damning. With it in the hands of the police, Clancy Snow was finished.

I had a weapon now, but how could I use it? Take it to the police myself? They might believe me, but there was always a possibility that it would take more than this evidence and my word to convict such an important civic figure as Clancy Snow. There were still plenty of gullible people around, unwilling to believe anything like this of him. And apart from that, he still had plenty of influence with the D.A.

I slipped the papers into an envelope, folded the flap, and stuck it down.

"Now we'll get out of here before we have any visitors." It was now nearly three o'clock. Things were likely to get a little unhealthy if we hung around the house much longer.

We walked out, down the wooden steps, on to the sand. I had one last thought about what would happen when the Big Men discovered the loss of the papers. Five, maybe six, of them were involved by name, the rest by implication. The pick-up order would be out with a vengeance within a few hours.

There were several dinghies drawn up on the sand, and the long pier was a great black snake stretching away into the night. Some of the bars were still open, lights blazing from windows. Clip-joints, many of them, paying their protection money to the syndicate, run by sharks who collected fancy dough from tourists and the kids down from L.A.

"What do we do now?"

I shrugged my shoulders. Did it matter much what happened after tonight, so long as these papers got into the right hands? For the first time since Maxie Temple had been shot at the airport, I could see a faint glimmer of success.

At least I was beginning to do something that wasn't dirty. It could mean landing myself with a murder rap, but first they'd have to stick the death of that hoodlum in the slum quarter on me.

But still, that was the it way went. In ten years of hanging around with the racketeers, rubbing shoulders with the toughs and the mobsters, some of the dirt was bound to rub off. It wasn't easy to fight back, make a stand, do something decent and clean for a change, especially when it meant spitting in the face of the Big Men and risking your neck to do it.

I'd made a whole world of enemies for myself. There were very few honest-to-goodness citizens who even recognised me, let alone considered me as a friend. Dawn was an exception to that, and I was grateful for it. But it had occurred to me that even she had an ulterior motive.

We reached Mike's car and it didn't look as though it had been spotted, but just to be on the safe side, we squinted in at the engine. It had been known for the Organisation to get rid of unwanted troublemakers by placing a home-made bomb in the car and rigging it up to the self-starter.

There wasn't anything there. Mike started up, edged carefully on to the road, and we headed back along Newport Beach in the direction of Los Angeles.

On the outskirts of Balboa, after traversing the Bay Avenue, in the main street, Mike stopped the car and looked across at me. The headlights were dipped, making a patch of brightness on the surface of the road.

"What is it, Mike?" I asked.

He licked his lips and ran his fingers over his face. He didn't answer.

I said again: "What's the matter, Mike?"

"This is as far as I can take you. I don't know where Clancy Snow is, but he's going to come running after you when he gets back and finds that safe busted and those papers gone. He'll put the finger on me for certain."

It seemed incredible, but I could see what he was getting at. Mike Spangler, unlike so many of the amateur cracksman, had his own technique, and that could be recognised.

After a minute, Mike leaned away from me. His voice was soft, but still lifeless.

"I understand, Mike," I said. "Thanks for the help, anyway."

"Any time."

I got out of the car. It was clear enough what he meant. It was also clear enough that unless I got out of that area pretty fast and back to Los Angeles, the entire night's work might be wasted.

I watched Mike turn the car and head back the way he had come. There was very little traffic on the road and what there was, was all heading in the wrong direction. Forty miles was a hell of a way to have to walk, especially at night and with an envelope in my pocket that spelled dynamite.

There was a kind of exhilaration deep inside me as

I started to walk. Not quite satisfaction, but something more. The knowledge that I had hit back at the men who had hounded me for the past four years, since San Quentin.

I wanted a drink, but it would have been dangerous. In my present mood, halfway between the peak of success and the depths of despair at not being able to get back into Los Angeles, I was liable to go off the deep end and drink myself stupid.

There was a neon sign outside one of the quieter joints that said 'Telephone' and I decided to call Dawn, to make sure that everything was all right back there. It occurred to me, standing there in the cool darkness, that if those guerrillas outside her place had miraculously moved on, she might be able to run out to Balboa and pick me up. Anyway, I thought, it was worth the risk.

I pushed open the door and went inside. The guy behind the bar gave me a funny look as I walked over the phone booth, then looked away and attended to his wiping. The slot took a handful of quarters for the call to Los Angeles. I could hear the burr of Dawn's phone.

It wasn't engaged, but nobody came to answer, and that had me more worried than anything else. Whatever happened now, I had to get back into Los Angeles. It was unlikely that Dawn would have gone out of her own accord and she was a pretty light sleeper, so the phone should have wakened her.

I went outside and started to walk. God alone knew what had happened at Dawn's place during the time

I had been away. I cursed myself for being such a damned fool as to have left her there, alone, with those hoodlums hanging about outside.

Clancy Snow would never have dared to rush the place during the daytime unless he was pretty desperate. But at night it was different.

I had began to feel little spasms running up and down my back and the fact that I was helpless to do anything made it worse than ever. The tough thing is when you finally realise what kind of a heel you really are. Here was I, Johnny Merak, self-styled white knight on a charger, thinking about myself so much, doing what I thought was all right for Johnny Merak, that I never gave a thought to what might happen to Dawn.

Twenty minutes later and a mile nearer to Los Angeles, I heard the rumble of a heavy truck approaching from the rear. Turning, I saw the headlights spearing along the curving road. One of the heavy cannery haulers heading for Los Angeles with a load of tuna.

I stepped out into the middle of the road. Once he stopped, it would be easy to persuade him to give me a lift as far as the city, even if I had to use a gun to do it, although that was something I didn't want to have to do unless it was absolutely necessary.

Action had to be the answer now. I waved my arms, feeling like a moth pinned in the headlights. There was a brief pain, a stabbing at the back of my eyes as the dazzling light threatened to blind me.

There was the harsh squeal of brakes against protesting tyres. The looming bulk of the vehicle was almost on me before it finally lurched to a standstill. The driver leaned down from the cab and peered at me in the darkness.

"Trying to get yourself killed, buster?" he asked harshly.

The buster talk had me cold, but I didn't show it. Maybe he thought I was some stupid drunk, working off the effects of a day's binge. Maybe he thought I was some tramp, hitching my way through the state for free.

"Can you give me a lift as far as Los Angeles?" I shouted back. It was difficult to see any details of him against the dark background of the cab.

I caught a glimpse of a brown leather jacket and a mop of dark hair above an unshaven face. He seemed to be trying to weigh me up.

"Get in," he said finally. "If you're only wanting to go through to Los Angeles, I guess I can take you that far."

"Thanks," I said, and released my hold on the .38 as I swung myself up beside him.

The truck nudged its way forward, seeming to drag itself behind the brilliant line of the headlights, probing the darkness in front of it. There was plenty of room in there, so I leaned back and scrutinised the driver without appearing too curious.

"You get stranded back there?" he asked finally, not once taking his eyes off the road.

"That's right. Missed the last bus. Important I get back to Los Angeles," I said.

"You're damned lucky, feller. There's never much traffic on this highway this early in the evening. I'm behind schedule myself."

We drove in silence for ten miles or so. Occasionally another car would pass us heading towards Balboa, filled with high-spirited kids who were determined to get the most out of life during their short stay at the coast.

We were headed west on the Hollywood freeway when we spotted the hold-up across the road. There were a couple of police cars and several cops milling around.

"Wonder what the hell this is?" mumbled the driver, roughly. He peered ahead through the windscreen. "Looks like a hold-up of some kind. Funny, I ain't never seen anything like this before in seventeen years of driving this route."

I thought fast. The idea occurred to me that Clancy Snow, realising that I had run out on him, slipped through his net of hirelings, had worked it so as to get a warrant issued for my arrest. He still held plenty of sway with the D.A.'s office and would undoubtedly continue to do so until these papers I had in my pocket were either published or handed over to a Federal Court.

The driver put his foot down on the brake and the vehicle started to slow. One of the cops had stepped out into the middle of the highway and was signalling us to stop and pulled into the kerb.

"Drive on, straight through them," I ordered.

The driver half-turned his head in surprise. "Are you crazy?" he muttered. "It's more than my licence is worth."

"You heard what I said. Put your foot down on the accelerator and ram that barricade. Hurry, or you'll regret it."

"Here! Just what's your game?" He turned his head fully for an instant, then saw the .38 in my hand. His eyes opened like a couple of eggs and his jaw dropped a couple of inches.

"Now, why not be smart?" I suggested, waving the gun threateningly. "And nobody is going to get hurt."

"I should have known better than to stop and give anybody a lift at this time in the morning. I might have known you'd be up to no good."

"Just get moving and leave the recriminations until later," I said. We were now within fifty yards of the barricade, and the cop was waving his arms frantically as the heavy truck thundered towards him.

He jumped for the kerb, split seconds before we hit the flimsy wooden barricade and splintered it to match-wood. Then we were through and there came a fusillade of shots from behind as we picked up speed. The rear driving-mirror tinkled into a shower of glittering fragments as a bullet hit it.

"Was all that really worth it?" muttered the driver after a brief pause, speaking through his teeth. "They'll get you in the end, however far you run, wherever you try to hide. Just what is it you are trying to prove? Why is it they're trying to pick you up?"

I kept the gun steady on him, just in case. "If you're that interested, I'll tell you. But I don't expect you to believe me. Ever heard of Clancy Snow? Dutch McKnight?"

"Sure, who hasn't? Big city financiers, aren't they?"

"Financiers? Don't kid yourself, either way, my friend. I know. I've been in their racket long enough to know what goes on behind the phoney elections, the propaganda speeches, and the swell dinners. I've got every bit of evidence necessary to blow them and their hoodlum empire sky-high. That's why they're doing everything in their power to stop me. Even that back there."

The driver laughed, big and loud. "You don't expect me to fall for that kind of talk, do you? If these guys are the crooks you make them out to be, how come the police are after you?"

"That's easy," I said cynically. "They've got the D.A. in their pockets, eating out of their hands. You don't think they'd have got to be where they are now unless they'd managed to swing an election for their particular candidate, do you?"

"You're lying," said the driver. There was disbelief in his voice.

"Careful what you say, friend," I warned. "Step out of line, and I may have to go on alone."

He shut up then and drove in sullen silence. Pretty soon we ran into the outskirts of Los Angeles. That was a little after five o'clock. The city was beginning to stir. Early morning traffic was already on the move.

Point of decision. I began to recognise the familiar landmarks. A quarter of a mile from Dawn's place I stopped him and got out. He eyed me sullenly from the cab.

"Thanks for the lift," I said, slipping the gun to my pocket. "I don't know what I'd have done if you hadn't happened along."

"Watch your step, mister," he said harshly. "I'll remember you and if I ever see you again without that gun I'll—"

"Get moving!" I said. "And don't stop if you know what's good for you."

Once again I felt like a heel. The white knight that had been Johnny Merak was slipping a bit. Going to Clancy Snow's secret hideout was in the way of a futile gesture, one that might or might not pay off.

I slowed down as I approached Dawn's place. The street at the front looked deserted on the surface. I hesitated at the end. It was unlikely that the Organisation had called off its hounds entirely. There would be some of them around, waiting for me to go back. Perhaps they were already in there, lurking behind the door, waiting for me to make a stupid mistake and walk in there with my eyes shut.

Still, there was nothing to be gained by standing around outside, like a fool. I walked forward slowly. A wrong move now might mean a hail of Tommy-gun bullets and an ex-crook lying dead in the gutter.

On the face of it, the house was empty. The door was half-open and silence lay at the back of it. I didn't shout Dawn's name. If she was there, alive, there was no need. If she wasn't, I would just give myself a way to anybody who might be waiting.

CHAPTER NINE
THE BIG FIX

The big room was both empty and dark, the curtain still drawn across the wide windows. Dawn was nowhere to be seen, but they hadn't taken her without a struggle. A couple of chairs lay on their sides and a framed picture hung lopsidedly on the wall.

I looked through the half-open door. There was a dim light on the stairs. I pushed the door open, kicking savagely at an overturned table that got in the way. There was a shoe on the stairs where Dawn had fought with the hoodlums as they had tried to hustle her off into the waiting car.

I was mad at myself. Mad for leaving her here to face this. Mad for being so stupid as not realising that this would inevitably happen. I had managed to escape the net and was still on the loose.

But how long will that last? That was something I didn't want to think about. I deliberately put it out of my mind. Dawn was a nice kid. Too nice for a thing like this to happen to her. There were a few like her still around in Los Angeles, fresh, innocent kids with the bloom of youth still on them, before they turned bitter with life.

Me? I'd been kicked about for eighteen years before I become a man and joined the mobs. The windows showed a grey glimmer as the sun began to come up over the city. A car went past and I sat up waiting for it to stop outside, but it just kept going, around the corner and away.

That's the worst part of sitting alone after pulling a job. Listening for the cars going by, never knowing when one was going to pull up and the heavy footsteps would come climbing the stairs, pausing outside the door.

Curiously, I wasn't afraid for myself any longer. And that, in itself, was a change for me. But I was mad, and it was a hell of a feeling. I knew what kind of man Clancy Snow was. A man with a big headache now that I knew how to put him and his henchmen on the spot for keeps. But he still had a trump card and I knew he'd use it.

Dawn Grahame.

He was the kind of man who would use every dirty trick in the game to stop me. And for good reasons.

I went into the kitchen and made myself a cup of coffee; black and strong. No sense in rushing into things. Maybe that was what they were hoping I'd do. Throw caution to the winds and go storming in there after Dawn with my eyes shut. If so, they were mistaken.

My face hurt and I felt as though I could sleep for a month. Instead, now was the time for action. I looked at myself in the mirror. My features were a mess. See if you can fix yourself out of this trap, Johnny, I thought bitterly.

I'd been used to eating alone, frequenting clip joints and cheap bars, but in the big room there, it was different. Lonely. Even in a couple of days, I'd grown used to seeing Dawn there, across the table from me.

The urge to get out and head like a madman for Balboa Bay exploded in me with an insane desire to kill Clancy Snow. But I had to sit back and think things out. For both our sakes, I had to get back into shape. My ribs still ached and there was a feeling of grit in my eyes and a fuzzy sensation inside my head that made thinking difficult.

I pulled out that leather envelope from my pocket and scanned through the papers again. Seen in the cold light of day, they made even more interesting reading them before. I sat there reading through them and was putting them carefully away again when the phone rang in the other room.

That sound did funny things to me. It wouldn't be Dawn calling.

I picked it up after a moment's pause. It could have been a trap to find out whether I was back. But I still had the papers, and for all they knew, I could have put them in a safe place.

At the moment, they were my only security, my only ticket to staying alive.

"That you, Merak?" Snow's voice was harsh and metallic.

"Sure," I said. "I've been expecting you to call. What's new?"

A pause, then: "You know dammed well why I'm calling you, Merak. We have got that girlfriend of yours as you probably have realised by now. She'll be well taken care of, believe me."

"I sincerely hope so, Clancy." I used his first name deliberately, goading him. It was like laughing in his face. "Otherwise some very important papers will find their way into the hands of the Federal Authorities."

"I don't understand the implication behind that statement." He was cautious. I had him on the hook and he knew it, but he wasn't going to let on. Not just yet. First he was going to find out just how much I really knew.

"You have got the message, all right," I told him. "That police hold-up from the Hollywood Freeway wasn't put there for my health. These papers are dynamite—you know what I mean—and if they get into the wrong hands, they can blow the lid right off this town."

"All right, Johnny. So you've got some papers." He didn't sound quite so sure of himself now. "What do you intend to do with them?"

"I could take them to the Federal Authorities."

His voice was like chipped ice now. "I wouldn't do that, if I were you. As you've guessed, they may be pretty important to us. I'll come clean with you. I can't talk too plain over the phone, you know that. Supposing I meet you somewhere, any place you care to mention, and we discuss this problem sensibly?"

"Are you kidding? Los Angeles isn't big enough for

me to find a place where I won't be bumped off by your boys. Do you think I'm crazy? I can see it all now. Me going there all trusting, expecting to have a nice, quiet chat with you—and what would happen?" I forced sarcasm into my voice. "You wouldn't be coming within a couple of miles of the place. I'd be picked up quietly, no fuss, either by your thugs or by the cops, and whichever way it happened, there'd be a one-way ticket to San Quentin at the end of it. I've seen it happen to too many guys that way before, Clancy, to fall for that one."

I was surprised he allowed me to finish. He seemed to be deliberating within himself, I heard the humming of the line, and then he said:

"Okay. I see your point. But don't forget we have the girl. You've seen what can happen to them, too, you know. These documents can ruin us and that isn't going to happen."

"Then what do you suggest?"

"I'll offer you a deal. Think it over carefully before you make up your mind."

"Go ahead," I said. "I'm listening." I hoped my voice didn't sound as jumpy as I felt.

"I don't know what you're trying to prove, Merak. You made a point of getting into my head ever since Maxie Temple was shot. You can smash us, but your girlfriend will die before that happens, and we'll get you if it's the last thing we do. You know that, don't you, Merak?"

Sure, he could do it. The word would go out and

I'd be riddled with bullets from a fast-moving car the moment I stepped onto the sidewalk.

One man against the entire Underworld of Los Angeles.

It didn't make sense. But I was doing it just the same. Going through with it for a girl with a pretty face and a fresh trust and innocence I hadn't known for a lifetime. Going through it because I'd had enough of the dirt and wanted to feel clean before it was too late.

And, finally, I was going through it for a guy named Johnny Merak, who had had a lot of senseless, stupid breaks, mostly because of his own fault, but who wanted to look his fellow men in the face again.

"Are you still there?" Clancy's voice against my ear.

"Sure, I'm listening."

"I'm willing to share the pot with you. No strings attached. You keep the papers that clear you and get the girl. In return, we want the rest of the documents from my safe. Is that a deal?"

"Okay," I said, speaking softly. "It's a deal."

I didn't trust him as far as I could throw him with one hand tied behind my back, but I needed to gain time. There was no intention in my mind of handing over those papers.

But now that I knew where Dawn was being held, or thought I did, I needed a few more hours to think things out and to do a bit of arranging.

"Good. Now you're talking sense. Where shall I meet you?"

"What about your place at Balboa?" I suggested.

I could almost hear his sharp intake of breath. That was the last place he had expected me to suggest. But he recovered quickly.

"That's fair enough by me," he said. "You will know where it is." He sounded tired but a little triumphant. No threat in his voice. Not now. But he was thinking so fast I could almost hear him. Wondering why I'd been fool enough to suggest his place. Probing for a deeper meaning behind my words.

"I'll be there," I said. "Make it early tomorrow morning, about three. And call off your dogs, Clancy, and the cops. Otherwise the deal's off."

"Sure. Sure. But don't try to cross us up, Johnny. You will regret it."

The phone clicked. I wiped the sweat from my forehead and wondered if I'd done the right thing. If it came off, all well and good. If it didn't, I was finished. And a good woman was finished, too.

I tried to get Mike Spangler on the line, but the voice of the other end said he was out, hadn't been in all day, and would I care to leave my name and they'd tell him to ring me back when he showed up. I hung up on that. The barman at that place was too nosy. Maybe even in Clancy Snow's pay. I knew then I'd have to play it alone.

I went back into the room, smoked a couple of cigarettes, and watched the street for the rest of the morning. For once, it seemed that Clancy had kept his word. The dogs had been called off. No keen-eyed gunmen on the street corner. Nothing.

By noon I decided he had fallen for the bait. He wouldn't hurt Dawn before I showed up with the papers. She was his only chance of getting them back and he knew it. For once, Clancy was facing stalemate. It must have been a new experience for a Big Man like him. Not being able to send out a couple of willing gunmen to fix things for him.

I made myself a bite of something to eat from the cans of food in the kitchen. On my wrist, the hands of my watch glided towards two o'clock. A whole host of little doubts were nibbling at the edges of my brain. There were so many things that could not be foreseen, that could so easily go wrong.

The entire scheme was crazy, utterly foolish. The afternoon went slowly. I tried to ring Mike Spangler again, but the answer was still the same, and the guy on the other hand was getting too suspicious for my liking.

Shortly before five, I slipped out of the side entrance into the garage at the back of the house. Dawn's car was still there, ready for a quick take-off. Everything looked normal, but I'd seen cars like that before, many times. Regular death-traps, waiting for an unsuspecting victim.

I lifted the bonnet, found the pair of slender wires running from the self-starter, merging expertly into the maze of wiring. Snipping them carefully, I pulled out the business end of the bomb. A cylindrical thing like the ones I'd seen before. One kick from the self-starter and I would have been blown to hell, with little enough remaining to identify me.

Clancy Snow didn't miss a trick, I thought cynically. I dumped the home-made bomb into a pail of cold water and left it there. It was harmless now; and there was a faint running of sweat on my back.

The Mercury started up easily. The deep-throated roar of pure power. There was plenty of juice in the tank. Deliberately, I took the long route through the quiet, deserted parts of Los Angeles. Dirty, tumbledown houses that dreamed in death. A handful of warehouses with hanging doors.

A couple of cabs passed me, cruising the streets like lost souls, looking for clients. They were unlikely to find many in this area. Here was the backwater of Los Angeles. Devoid of life. Aged people in doorways. Empty, staring windows. Broken panes, broken lives, broken dreams.

Men and women living in a twilight world with no hope, scraping a bare existence from their surroundings. A row of saloons licensed for the sale of hard liquor, providing one form of solace and forgetfulness from the world. A place of forgotten people who didn't really want to be forgotten, but who couldn't help it.

I was glad when I finally hit the highway on the edge of town and left it all behind me. The needle of the speedometer wavered around the fifty mark and I kept it there with my foot on the accelerator. Not too fast, because I still had plenty of time to kill.

Five-thirty and I reached the place where the roadblock of the night before had been. There was no sign of it now. The cops had been busy, jumping to an order from the D.A., who had himself jumped to a similar order from Clancy Snow.

I swung that Mercury around a sharp bend in the road. It was good to be alone in the car. Good, because I had to think and think first. I hung onto the wheel, disregarding my aches and pains and the fact that I'd had no sleep for almost thirty hours.

I wondered what Clancy and Dutch McKnight were doing. They'd be in on this together. It didn't just affect Clancy Snow. All of the Big Bosses of the Organisation were facing defeat and exposure if I got through with these documents. For the first time, I realised just how important I really was.

It gave me a clean, warm feeling inside, just to think about it. They would all be running now as they had never run before: milling around like rats. Hurried telephone conversations. The sleek Cadillacs racing out to their headquarters. Hoping against hope that I'd been stupid enough for once and not checked for the bomb in the car. They'd know by now that I hadn't fallen for it. I only hoped that, somehow, Dawn knew it, too. It might give her something to hold on to.

Melodrama, Johnny, nothing but melodrama. It was and it wasn't. Not with a dammed nice kid holed up in that beach house. She hadn't really known how hard and cruel and dirty the world really was; she'd soon find out.

Inside, I was feeling both good and bad. Good because, at last, I was doing something decent instead of sitting around as I had all day. Bad, because I had the jitters and was trying unsuccessfully to hide the fact, even from myself. My sweat-soaked clothes were sticking to my body. The road was a long empty stretch of front of me, blazing in the evening sunlight.

I ran the Mercury into the main street in Balboa shortly after six o'clock. The evening traffic was beginning to get heavy and I had to go slowly, cutting through it. The beaches were crowded, packed with couples in swimming trunks and coloured beachwear. All of this suited my purpose.

I parked the car outside Christian's and went inside for a drink. Not that I really needed one, but I had to stay out of sight until it was dark. And the best way to do that in a large place like Balboa was to mix with the crowds.

A radiogram was going full blast from one of the other rooms. Smooth south-sea-island stuff. At least, it was in keeping with the surroundings. I figured it would be dark enough for my purpose about nine-thirty, perhaps a little before. Until then, I had to keep out of sight and that was important.

I sat sipping my drink, watching the bar fill up behind me, scanning the faces through the crystal mirror that ran the full length of the room behind the bar. There were some faces that were vaguely familiar, but they were all from a long way back, seven years or more. I felt reasonably safe. They wouldn't recognise me now.

A woman was crooning in a husky voice over by the piano. A tall woman in an evening gown, her mouth a splash of scarlet across her white, powdered features. This would be the stop-gap act before the real floor-show.

Through the wide windows I could see the rim of the ocean with the painted boats bobbing up and down like corks on the water. Plenty of money to burn and only a few crowded weekends in which to do it. That was the way it always was at Balboa.

Which was the main reason why crooks like Clancy and Dutch managed to pull in such big rake-offs from the mugs. I'd been in that racket ones, but thanks to having looked right inside a guy named Johnny Merak and not liking what I saw, I'd gone a long way towards finishing with it.

The sun was going down now, almost hidden behind the horizon. There were a few clouds and there might be a moon, and that made things difficult.

Dawn had it right. There was no sense in keeping running because, in the end, there was nowhere else to run, and you found that the only guy you couldn't run away from was—yourself. But there was also no sense in starting some shooting vendetta with these guys.

They all had to be put away at one and the same time. If they weren't, there was no place I could hide where they wouldn't find me, some day, some year.

While I'd been thinking, another part of my brain had been busy watching the faces of the people coming in. Christian's was a popular place on the beach. At some time or another everybody who was anybody came there.

I saw the smallish guy come in and watched him as he made his way across the floor towards the other end of the bar. He walked like a dancer, as though his feet were on little springs, his body swaying from side to side. And his eyes were never still, probing everybody, flicking from side to side, careful and alert.

I turned my head and buried my face in my class. Here was one guy I didn't want to see. Alfred Madden. Gunman for Dutch McKnight. So the big fish were moving them in fast. Soon the place would be crawling with them, blocking every road out to Clancy Snow's beach house, waiting for me to show up.

Maybe they'd jump me the minute they spotted me; or, maybe, they'd be content to watch me blunder along, until I got there and they were ready to receive me.

I was glad now that I hadn't brought the papers with me. The leather envelope was in my pocket all right, but it wouldn't do them any good to get their hands on that. The papers inside were more than useless.

Madden draped himself across a still and gave his order in a low voice to the barman. He never once gave me a second glance and I began to feel safe again. It wasn't likely that they would expect me to walk into Balboa like this. They'd expect me to creep in like a defeated rat.

A crowd of kids came in a couple of minutes later and packed the bar between Madden and myself and I lost sight of him. There was a sound of high-pitched feminine laughter. I stayed there for twenty minutes and three drinks, then left and walked along the sand dunes.

I could just make out Clancy's beach house house in the distance, standing by itself, raised a little above the surrounding ground. He'd chosen it well. Easy to defend and easy to spot intruders a mile away.

I had the uneasy feeling that they had binoculars on me, watching me over a distance of a couple of miles, but I shook it off.

It wasn't going to be an easy pitch. In the darkness it might be possible to get there without being seen; and it might also be possible to get Dawn out without getting ourselves killed in the attempt. But we had to get back to the car and by that time the alarm would have been given.

It was a pity I couldn't take the cart nearer their beach house, but that was impossible. Whoever had planted the bomb in it had taken a dammed a good look at it; if it was spotted and recognised, it wouldn't be there when we came out with a rush and wanted it.

No, it wasn't going to be easy, even if I got all the breaks. But whatever I did, whatever happened, I'd have one big advantage on my side.

They were expecting me to call at three o'clock in the morning. They'd be ready for me by then.

But I was going in before midnight, three hours early.

CHAPTER TEN
THE RAT-HOLE

The beach house, standing on the rising knoll of ground, was as dark as when I had last seen it with Mike Spangler. An unimaginative two-storey building, wooden-walled with a sloping roof. Curtains had been drawn across the window so that they looked like blind eyes staring sightlessly across the sand dunes.

I was within twenty yards of the rear entrance before I spotted the first of Clancy's watchdogs. A dark shadow that moved and thereby distinguished itself from the background.

This was the showdown and I didn't waste any time.

The .38 had a silencer, but even that made a sound in the stillness of this place, and Clancy's men were reputed to have sharp ears. Holding it by the barrel, I brought it down sharply behind the other's left ear. The hoodlum collapsed without a sound, falling onto the sand that muffled any noise his body might have made.

There was another guy at the corner of the house, but he'd neither seen nor heard anything, and was still standing there as solidly as ever as I approached the back door. It was locked as I had anticipated it would be, but having picked a lock before, it took me a mere few seconds to open it.

I stepped forward into darkness and a silence that was only broken by the eternal dripping of a tap somewhere. I figured that this was the kitchen, but it was almost impossible to see anything.

Gingerly, I walked forward, one hand outstretched in front of me. This was perhaps the trickiest part of the whole operation. In my mind's eye, I could see Clancy and his men, sitting somewhere in the darkness within twenty feet of me, watching their hands on the luminous dials of their watches creep slowly towards three o'clock.

There was an impatience within me that was hard to control. My nerves were all on edge, screaming at the silence, waiting for the slightest sound.

On the other side of the kitchen I found a door. I stopped and held my breath. Still nothing moving.

I was just beginning to think that the place was deserted and that I'd walked into some trap with a bomb sitting in the cellar waiting to go off at the first wrong move I made, when I heard a noise.

I balanced the gun in my right hand and pushed the door wider. That noise had done funny things to my heart beats and sent a column of nervous shocks parading up and down my spine. I couldn't place it, but it sounded like a low moan. And it came from the room above my head.

Slowly my eyes were becoming accustomed to the darkness. I had a pencil torch in my pocket, but I didn't want to use it unless it was strictly necessary. I was right in the middle of the rat-house, sitting in the middle of the headquarters of the biggest group of racketeers Los Angeles had known for several decades.

I slipped through the door, found myself at the bottom of a fight of carpeted steps. They led upwards into darkness and silence.

Well, there was nothing for it. There could be a thug hiding behind every corner, on the bend in the stairs, at the top, outside the door behind which Dawn was locked.

I started up them, praying that none of the treads would creak when I put my weight on it. I checked the eagerness of my stride as I reached the top. So far, so good.

I checked my watch. A little after ten. Not much time left. They'd be getting ready for me, preparing the trap, ready to spring it as soon as I walked in through that door at the front. I'd seen part of it as I entered. The hoodlum waiting in the grounds. The quiet shadows that moved silently, alert and watchful.

I thought, too, of that unconscious thug lying out there in the bushes, face downwards in the sand. It was only a matter of minutes before he was found. And if Dawn and I weren't safely out of the house by then, we were finished.

The rustle came again, followed by the faint moan of pain, rather as though she had a gag over her mouth and was trying to cry out.

I listened outside the nearest door. Not a sound from

inside. I tried the next. It was locked. I turned the handle slowly, paused as I heard the sound again.

The lock was tricky. A new one. It took the best part of five minutes to pick it, but finally the door opened with a slight snap.

I had to use the pencil torch then. If there was a guard inside the room, it would be just too bad, but I didn't think so. If they had placed a guard there, it was unlikely they would also have locked the door.

I saw her in the round splash of light where the beam struck. She was lying on the bed over against the wall, her arms and legs bound with thin cord that would cut into the flesh whenever she moved. I came up to her gently and whispered: "It's all right, Dawn. It's me, Johnny." I could see the surprise in her eyes. They dilated in the light from the torch and I swung the beam away, loosening the gag from around her mouth.

"Johnny! Thank God you came! What happened?"

"I'll explain later, Dawn," I whispered. "We're still not out of danger. This place is crawling with Clancy Snow's hoodlums. They've been arriving here all day. They're worried."

She sat up, rubbing her wrists where red weals showed how the cord had bitten deep into them.

"Think you can stand up by yourself?"

"I'll try. I think so." She got to her feet and stood swaying for a brief moment while she held on to my arm.

Maybe only a few minutes before that unconscious thug was either discovered or regained consciousness and opened his mouth loud enough for everybody in the vicinity to hear.

There came the sound of movement and harsh voices from downstairs. Had that guy been found already? A frenzy of urgent excitement exploded inside my brain, propelling me towards the door, dragging Dawn behind me.

Somebody came lunging out of a door at the bottom of the flight of stairs, silhouetted against a flood of light. Whoever he was, he seemed to be drunk. There was a bottle in his hand, a curse on his lips.

Someone else shouted something unintelligible from the room he had just left. I pressed back against the wall, feeling the door hard against my back, holding my breath until it hurt. I could feel Dawn trembling beside me.

That had been Clancy's voice, yelling from the room. So the King Rat was here with his men. Not wanting to have anything go wrong with his plans, he had decided to come in person.

But he wouldn't expose himself to danger. Johnny Merak, if he turned up at three o'clock as arranged, would be disarmed and harmless before Clancy made his appearance.

I tried to think as I watched the drunk stagger towards the kitchen. A moment later the outer door closed loudly. Giving him half a minute to get well away, we crept down the stairs.

It gave me a peculiar feeling in the pit of my stomach to realise that Clancy Snow and possibly Dutch

McKnight were in the other room, within ten feet of others, planning my demise.

In a few seconds we were outside. It seemed incredible that our luck had held, but the trickiest part was now past. Dawn was a different woman now. Some of the fear had been wiped from her features. She looked more composed now.

The breeze, blowing off the Pacific, was cool in our faces. There was still a little of the nameless terror inside me as we headed away from the beach house. Shadows became things that stopped us in our tracks, brought our hearts thudding into our throats. Part of the way we ran, stumbling over the sand. Mostly we walked, doubled up, to present the most difficult target for the bullets I kept thinking was coming our way.

It just didn't seem possible. That I had gone into Clancy Snow's headquarters and stolen his precious captive from under his very nose. It wasn't like Fate to deal me breaks like that.

"What happened, Dawn?" I asked breathlessly, when we were at the best part of a quarter of a mile away. Still over a mile to go before we reached the car, but I felt reasonably safe for the first time that day.

"I don't really know. I stayed there like you said until almost eleven o'clock. I wanted to be with you, Johnny; and when the phone rang and somebody who said he was a friend of yours told me you had been run down by a hit-and-run driver and were calling for me at the hospital, I went. They must have been waiting for me in their garage. Something hit me at the back of the neck and I must have passed out. When I came round, I found myself in that room. It was almost daylight, so I guessed I'd been out for several hours."

She turned her head and looked at me for several minutes before going on.

"But what I still don't understand is how you knew where to find me. What is that place, Johnny?"

"That? Clancy Snow's headquarters. I knew how to find it for the simple reason that I was there last night."

"So that's why they were so mad when they discovered you'd run out on them." Dawn was close, her words almost a whisper.

"Yes."

"They were waiting for you in that place. One of them kept telling me that you'd be there at three o'clock in the morning, but that you'd never stand a chance of getting out alive." Her voice was flat with an edge of bitterness. "Now what, Johnny? I suppose I loused things up for you."

"You weren't to know, Dawn," I said. "But we're going to have to get out of here and fast. Once we are in Los Angeles, I intend to fix things for Snow and his friends so that he won't be doing anything for a hell of a time."

"What do you mean?"

"To start with, I went to that beach house last night to get those papers. I had a hunch Snow might have them once Maxie Temple was killed. He wouldn't pass up on a deal like that. Maybe he figured he could get me to work with him, if he held them over my head."

"And you managed to find them?"

"I got them, all right. And others besides. Enough to blow the top off Snow's rackets. That's why he had his men take you along. To force my hand and get me to make a deal with him—you in return for the papers. I had him on the phone this morning. That's why I arranged to meet him there at three o'clock this morning. What he didn't know was that I intended to turn up several hours earlier."

She was looking at me, trying to see my face in the darkness. "You really mean to get them all, don't you?"

"That's right," I said. "This morning, when I found they'd taken you, I did a good deal of thinking. In particular, I thought about myself. The kind of guy I am and the kind I'd like to be. They weren't nice thoughts."

"No, Johnny. But they were honest ones. Maybe for the first time in your life you were being honest with yourself."

Coming from anybody else I'd have rammed my fist in their face for saying that, but from Dawn, the words sounded good.

I opened my mouth to say something more, but it was never said. Because at that moment every light in that beach house seemed to come on, lighting it up so that it could be seen for miles.

Without pausing to think, I grabbed Dawn's hand and hurried her across the soft sand.

I didn't say anything, but I think she knew what had happened. Our escape had been discovered. The rats were on the move!

CHAPTER ELEVEN
THE SWITCH

Dawn's car was where I had left it, parked in front of Christian's ready for a quick getaway. There were no others blocking the way.

"Quickly! Inside!" I said harshly. "I'd better drive. This is going to be rough."

I had my fingers on the ignition key when a remembered voice close to my ear said: "Don't bother to start her up, Merak. You're not going anywhere. Clancy Snow wants to see you. Both of you."

It was Alfred Madden.

"I've wanted to meet up with you all day, Merak." His voice was low and soft, taunting.

There was a rush of thoughts piling through my mind as I sat there, looking at him. The minutes and the precious seconds were ticking away, and if those cars from the beach house caught up with us, we'd be finished even before we'd started.

"What's this with you, Madden?" I asked, keeping my voice quiet. "You working for Clancy, too?"

"I never did like you, Johnny," he said thinly, still smiling. "That's why I'm doing this, okay?"

"Sure," I said, "if that's the way you want it." I opened the door of the car sharply, unexpectedly, butting him with it in the pit of the stomach. The gun in his hand went rolling onto the gravel as he lurched backwards, off balance.

Maybe I was wrong in deciding to finish him there and then; perhaps I should have stayed in the car, backed it out, and gone while he lay floundering on the ground. But his gun was still there within easy reach, and he could have dropped us both before we were ten yards away.

His left fist was coming up in a streaking punch for my face as I rushed him. Ducking, the blow grazed over my shoulder and my head caught him in the chest. We went over backward, arms locked, Madden underneath.

He broke my fall. Outwardly he was only a little guy, but hard as nails, with a surprising strength and agility in his wiry body. I crashed into him with my right fist again and we rolled into the gravel.

His arm swung downwards in a shallow arc, hammering into my cheek. Pain jarred redly through the muscles of my face and neck. He tried again, but I was already twisting and his bunched fist missed by barely an inch.

Out of the corner of my eye I could see his fingers scrabbling for the gun, touching, closing over the butt. Once he got that I was finished. A heel came down on his outstretched fingers, grinding them into the gravel. He let out a grunt of pain as Dawn went and picked up the gun.

At the same time I hammered a wild swing at his ribs, but he was dropping back as it landed, catching him full in the throat, knocking the wind from him.

He fell back, moaning and gasping, kicking and retching as he went down. There was a murderous glint in his close-set eyes. This man was out to kill me no matter what.

I kicked him hard in the ribs, and saw that he was finished. Running for the car, I slipped in behind the wheel, surprised to find that Dawn was already there, waiting.

My head was spinning madly and there was blood, tasting salt, on my lips. I wiped them hastily with a handkerchief, but I wasn't thinking about my particular aches and pains at that moment.

Somewhere in the near distance there was the sound of powerful cars racing towards the scene. In them would be men driven by the insane urge to kill. I jabbed the self-starter, backed the Mercury off the kerb, felt the bump as we hit the road, spun the wheel savagely, and gunned her away from Balboa. I was trembling all over, shaking with suppressed nervous tension.

Dawn glanced over her shoulder at the road behind us, stretching away like a ribbon of darkness along the shore of the Pacific. Then she looked back at me, questioningly.

"You nearly killed him, Johnny," she said.

"That's right. If I hadn't, he'd have killed me, all right," I mumbled. My lips seemed to be swollen to twice their normal size, but I wasn't caring so long as I could keep the Mercury on the road and ahead of those Cadillacs behind us.

"That little man was Alfred Madden." There was no question in Dawn's voice; it was just a statement of fact.

"Right first time," I mumbled. "Remember how he treated his girlfriend, Cleo Newton? A man like that has no soul. He'd be better off dead."

I relapsed into silence. It was difficult to talk with fire blazing along the muscles of my face and an icy feeling on the back of my neck as I visualised Clancy Snow's men drawing closer on our tail.

I couldn't see them in the driving mirror, but if they had any sense they'd have the headlights dipped, the glare reducing so as to be on us before we realised it.

The speedometer needle crept up to seventy and stayed there. We roared through a clover-leave inter-section just beyond Newport. Fortunately, there was very little traffic on the road at this time of night and there was a moon high up, above a ridge of white cloud, making it possible to see some little way ahead.

I knew this stretch of the road like the back of my hand. Tyres screamed thinly as we rounded a sharp bend, clawed at the road and held miraculously.

Dawn's face was white, but she was taking it well. She'd been through a hell of a lot these past couple of days. So had I for that matter, but I was used to it; she wasn't.

"They're gaining on us," she said suddenly, speaking

through her tightened lips. She was scared to pieces, but determined not to show it.

I threw a swift glance in the rear driving-mirror. The nearest car was a black shadow, sleek and powerful, less than a quarter of a mile behind us and coming up fast. There were at least three others at the back of us.

The rats were out with a vengeance. This is what they really live for; the chase and the kill at the end of it.

"Better keep your head down, Dawn," I warned. "They may start shooting as soon as they're within range."

She was silent for a long moment, then asked another question. A tough one.

"Do you think we'll make it, Johnny?"

"Sure," I said, lying in my teeth. "We'll make it, unless they've been thinking ahead all the time and have got more roadblocks set up between here and Los Angeles. Somehow I don't think that's likely."

"I hope you're playing it straight with me," she murmured softly, biting her lower lip. "Because I don't think I could stand any more lies and half-truths."

"All right. We don't stand much of a chance, but I'm going to get you out of this mess, if it's the last thing I do."

"That's not going to be easy, unless you have got something figured out." She was looking at me, trying to see the expression on my face, I guess. I didn't like lying to her. I'd lied to plenty of dames before, but that had been different somehow.

We roared along the northbound freeway, slid between a couple of slower-moving cars, heard the indignant blast of protest die away behind me into the distance. We were now out of the mainstream of Los Angeles-bound traffic and in a comparatively deserted lane.

"It doesn't look as though we're going to shake them off our tail," said Dawn, as we swung round a corner, cutting the roadside dangerously close.

But it had to be like this now; the risks had to be taken. Clancy Snow would be mad now. A dangerous man, intent on revenge. He had been made to look like a fool by someone he considered to be nothing more than a cheap crook. It would rankle.

Little thoughts were buzzing around in my head as I tried to concentrate on driving. I had the envelope— but what good did that do me now? They'd kill us both and ask questions later.

Snow wasn't a fool. He'd have kept a strict watch on me back at Dawn's place, even though I hadn't spotted any of his boys. The reception that Dawn had spoken of, waiting for me at the beach house for three o'clock, had shown quite clearly that he had no more trusted me than I trusted him.

He'd know, for sure, that I hadn't had a chance to put those papers in a strongbox, so they had to be either on me or in the house in Los Angeles. Either way, he didn't need me alive to get them.

I wished I hadn't been so stupid not to have thought of that before. While all this was going on in my mind,

I was aware of the cars drawing nearer on our tail. There wasn't much traffic in front of me, and I swung the Mercury from side to side, to present a more difficult target to the gunmen, who would be studying their .38s, fingers itching on the triggers.

Dawn smiled, a nice smile. All of the bitterness and the fear seemed to have melted away. She wasn't a frightened kid any longer. She was a woman, and she knew what would happen if those hoodlums caught up with us; and she wasn't afraid.

Above the muffled roar of the engine, I heard a crack and a drone like an angry bee close to my ear. A neat hole with a sprinkling of cracks appeared in the windscreen in front of me.

"Get down!" I shouted.

Dawn looked startled, but obeyed.

The car began to lurch a little as the speedometer needle touched eighty. The road turned slightly and I edged the wheel round. The headlights picked up objects some thirty or forty yards ahead, but that wasn't far enough at the speed we were travelling.

There was a wild blare of horns at the back of us. The first Cadillac was less than twenty feet away, coming up fast. I could just see a figure leaning from the side, glimpsed the faint spit of flame an instant before I heard the bark of the gun.

But I was already side-slipping the car and the bullet went past us into the night.

"Look out!" Dawn screamed, lifting her head, as the Cadillac edged up alongside, trying to force me off the road.

I pulled the wheel over, hard, swinging into the middle of the lane. That was the only way to deal with a move like this. The Cadillac lurched as the driver fought to regain control. He hadn't expected that move and it must have unnerved him sufficiently for the trick to work.

Gently, I swung him further over towards the left-hand edge of the road. Out of the corner of my eye I could glimpse a driver fighting to swing the car straight, but he had left it too late.

The subdued glare of his dipped headlights limned the low wall at the bend some twenty yards ahead. He never stood a chance. The bonnet seemed to come up of its own accord, wheel spinning, clawing the air.

Breathing heavily, I slewed the wheel round, straightened the Mercury and felt the tyres grip the road surface again. It had been a close thing. Too close for my liking.

Dawn covered her face with her hands and didn't look. I caught a fragmentary glimpse of the Cadillac jumping the road, smashing into the wall head-on, piling high in a blur of folding steel.

It was all over in twenty seconds, but it had been sufficient to give us the breathing space I needed. The next car was more than two hundred yards to the rear, and although he was coming up fast and had disregarded the wreckage, there was still time.

"Listen, Dawn," I said in a hoarse, hurried whisper, "and don't argue. This is the only chance we're likely to get. Things are too hot for you to be involved. This is what we're going to do."

Headlights brightened the road ahead of me and I was blinded for a brief moment.

"There's a sharp turn less than half a mile ahead. I'll slow down as I reach it. Be ready to open the door and jump out. There's a grass verge, so you should be okay. Once you hit the ground, roll over fast and get out of sight. I'll try to lead them away."

"No, Johnny. I'm sticking with you. I got you into this mess and I'm not running out on you now."

"Listen: do as I say. I'll be okay. But I can't think straight with you here. I'm thinking about you all the time instead of those hoodlums behind us. You've got to do as I say. Get it?"

"All right, if that's the way you want it." Her voice was tired and lifeless.

The bend showed up in the headlights; a sharp turn. The car began to careen as I hit the brakes, but she responded slowly. The speedometer dropped crazily, wavered, then stuck around the fifteen mark.

I edged in towards the grass verge. Dawn had the door open and a blast of cold night air struck me forcibly, chilling my back and chest as it tore through my sweat-soaked clothing.

"Ready, Dawn?" I yelled.

She nodded. Her face was white and she was deliberately bracing himself. We were going slow now, just edging out of sight of the boys behind.

"Right!"

She jumped and I saw her roll over several times, and then get up and run down out of sight. I jammed on the gas. They hadn't seen the switch. When they came into sight again, they were less than fifty yards away.

CHAPTER TWELVE
CHASE

It was good to be there by myself, without Dawn. She was safe now, no matter what happened to me. Another long stretch of road and at the end of it darkness, where the headlights wouldn't reach.

The switch had lost me a hundred yards. It was giving away too much. The Mercury was good, but it couldn't stand the pace with the Cadillacs.

Another sharp crack and a bullet that went by me in the darkness so that it was impossible to tell whether it had missed me by an inch or several feet.

I wondered if there was a future in what I was doing. Whether this white knight game wasn't just a little beyond the efforts of Johnny Merak. I didn't seem to be making out too well in this new role.

I took a tight grip on the wheel and felt it slipping against the palms of my sweating hands. I'd had Clancy Snow and the others right where I wanted them, or so I'd thought. I'd applied a nice piece of elementary psychology that Snow would have been too dumb to think of, and his plan had cracked in half like a rotten biscuit.

Yes, I'd certainly been one of the bright boys, all right! The only thing I hadn't bargained for was what was actually happening now. I swung the car forward into the night and thought some more.

I didn't doubt any longer that Snow had arranged the killing of Maxie Temple. Everything fitted in too nicely for it to be otherwise. But there were still several suspects. Madden: he was the most likely. He was a man who didn't need a motive; he didn't even need to know the guy he was to kill. All he wanted was the money.

Dutch McKnight himself: he was a Big Man, but had been known to fix things personally. I thought some more and, strangely enough, I found my thoughts wandering around to Cleo Newton.

A woman like Dawn in certain respects. She, too, lived in a private hell. But hers was one peopled by the wild, incredible phantoms of her own drug-crazed brain. From what I'd seen of her in that dingy flat, her periods of comparative sanity weren't frequent or long.

But the craving would undoubtedly be strong enough for her to kill for more heroin. In that condition, she would do anything she was told. What better killer to have? Madden would have attracted as much attention as a two-headed circus freak on Balboa Beach, but Cleo Newton, she would be able to slip in there unnoticed, fire the killing shot, and get out again before anyone knew what had happened.

The more I thought about it, the more it figured. I could have gone on thinking along those lines for quite a while, only I realised what kind of a fix I was in myself. I could feel the sweat streaming off my forehead.

This time, when I looked into the rear driving-mirror, I saw that one of the Cadillacs was so close he was almost touching my back bumper.

I pushed my foot down and started accelerating. The Mercury drew ahead a little way, but the other guy hung on grimly. He'd obviously seen what had happened to his companion and he didn't want to come too close unless he was sure of himself.

I rounded a long curve. The lights of Los Angeles were a faint, bright ribbon far below me. The car was lurching madly now, tyres screaming on the road. Eighty on the speedometer and creeping up slowly.

I wanted to laugh out loud at the idea of Clancy Snow, thinking Dawn Grahame was still with me in the car, urging his men on to the kill, but the effort of moving my bruised jaw was too much.

I didn't hear the shot behind me that burst the rear offside tyre, but I knew when it hit. The Mercury tilted, careened wildly, began to swing. I fought desperately to keep her under control, trying to straighten the wheel. I hit the curve ahead far too fast to ever hope to make it.

The grass verge swung up in the blaze of the headlights, every detail etched clear in my brain. There was a flimsy wooden fence at the top and I went ploughing through it. Miraculously, the car was still straight as I hit the top of the verge. Then I was over and she started to turn, throwing me against the wheel and the dash-board.

There was a brief blaze of stars and then darkness.

I must have taken a long while fighting my way back to consciousness. My head was humming with reaction and there was a blinding glare in front of my eyes that wouldn't go away no matter how I twisted my face. Stabs of pain knifed through my brain. I tried to move but my legs refused to obey me.

I opened my eyes, and then shut them again, fast, almost blinded. I wasn't dead. My entire body ached but I was still alive. Until I heard the voice from the back of the light and I knew that, whatever happened, I wouldn't be alive much longer.

"You led us quite a chase, Johnny." Dutch McKnight. So he'd come out into the open at last. The big executive from Los Angeles. The guy who arranged the top-level deals for the businessmen. The eminent citizen, charitable, generous, filled with the milk of human kindness. The election man.

The cheap racketeer!

I could feel the ruthless edge of cruelty in his voice and compared him with Clancy Snow, wondered which of the two was the worse. But that latent cruelty was part of his strength. Without it, and the fear it produced, he and the others would be little men of no account. They relied entirely on fear and threats and bribes and extortion. Nothing else.

"Johnny, can you hear me?"

I couldn't see him for the red glare cutting into my

eyes, searing into my brain even through the lids when I screwed them up tight. I nodded my head, wincing as pain lanced into my shoulder muscles.

"Good." He spoke softly with a trace of accent. "I understand you have some important papers belonging to us. We want them back. And fast. You understand?"

"You don't say."

A quiet chuckle from the darkness at the back of the light.

"Bravely said, Johnny. But we haven't got too much time for heroics. You were a mess when we pulled you out of that wrecked car. Unfortunately, you didn't have the papers with you; that's the only reason why you're alive now. I presume you left them in a safe place?"

A leading question. I nodded. "I left them somewhere you'll never live to lay your hands on them," I said.

"I don't think so, Merak." Clancy Snow's voice, harder and more sinister. He sounded impatient. An impatient guy who wanted to get things done.

Gradually, my eyes became more accustomed to the glare, and I could just make out the figures at the back of it. Snow, standing over by the wall, pale eyes watching me, blond hair glinting in the light. He watched me dispassionately, like an entomologist might look at a prize specimen, stuck to a block with a pin.

Dutch McKnight was seated at the table, giving away his nervousness by the insistent drumming of his fingertips on the polished wood. Small, tubby guy, muscular once, but going to fat. Thinning hair and a stubby moustache that seemed the hallmark of a successful crook.

Unlike Snow, he didn't deliberately keep himself in the background of civic affairs. You could see McKnight any day of the week, hobnobbing with the big shots of city life, the upper social sphere, among the elected representatives of the people.

He had never been known to stand for any office himself but preferred to pull the strings from behind the scenes. Making the puppets dance to any tune he called. Most of the time he'd managed to keep himself clean of any convictions. There had been talk in their downtown bars, but it was difficult to pin down.

"It would be easier all round if you decided to talk." Dark eyes watching me, noticing every movements of my features; calm voice speaking hurriedly, as if he had all the time in the world.

"Why?"

"Because we can always break you down the end. You'll talk then. Why not do it now and save yourself all that unnecessary beating?"

I could see the thugs in the background, two gorillas near the door, another leaning against the wall. Their faces seemed alive with a dreadful hunger, eyeing me, waiting to get their teeth into me.

Professional men with a lifetime of experience at the back of them. Hand-picked. The scum of Los Angeles, Detroit, Chicago, and any other place you cared to name.

There was more than physical threat here in spite of

the forced calm and gentleness in McKnight's voice. He wasn't an idiot, an utter fool. He knew he had to get his hands on those papers or he and the Organisation were as good as finished.

But he wouldn't force things along as Snow wanted to do.

He leaned forward suddenly, tilting the light a little to the left so that it no longer shone full in my face and there was a dancing green haze hovering in front of my aching eyes.

"Between friends," he began softly, "just what did you expect to get out of all this? Why did you suddenly start this one-man campaign against the Organisation? It was only after Maxie had been killed that you began this idiotic crusade. You weren't that fond of Temple to want to get yourself killed for avenging his death. I'll never be able to understand your motives, Merak."

I kept my mouth shut. The 'friend' bit had me cold, but I gave no sign. Besides, how do you explain to a guy like McKnight that you hate his guts and those of his whole rotten set-up; that you want to smash them for good and all, even if it means smashing yourself in the process? The answer was, that you didn't. So I didn't answer him.

"Not inclined to talk, Johnny?" Snow stepped forward, anger and impatience written all over his sallow features, but McKnight waved him back.

"He's going to talk, Clancy, don't worry about that."

I heard the words and I guessed exactly at the meaning behind them. Nobody could face up to the might of the Underworld Organisation and hope to win through in the end. It just wasn't possible. My little effort was nothing more than a scratch on the surface.

The underworld was too big, too widespread, like a giant octopus, growing stronger and larger on the fear of little men. Fed and nurtured by the paid hit-and-run drivers, the unexpected stream of bullets sprayed from a fast-moving sedan.

Informers didn't last long in Los Angeles. Traitors and do-gooders like myself had even shorter lives as a general run. There was a host of broken men and women in the city can testify to that from personal experience.

"What makes you so sure I'll talk?" I asked. It was the wrong question. I could see it in McKnight's eyes. The way they narrowed into mere slits, leaving the rest of his face unchanged.

A low laugh came from one of the thugs near the door. An ugly sound. The kind of sound one would expect evil to make.

"You're a dammed fool, Merak. But time's getting tight. We want those papers and you know where they are. Why try to be clever? It won't get you anywhere."

A quiet voice with no threats in it. Friendly, like a rattler just before it strikes, lulling its victim into an hypnotic state of false security. The words were very low, soft.

"I'm a pretty poor bargain, McKnight," I said. He didn't move so much as a muscle. "Not a good guy when it comes to doing something decent, I'm afraid.

But I had to do what I did—all of it—but I've also got the dope on you and that's what counts in the end."

"Is it? Don't forget that we picked the girl up once, we can do it again, if necessary. Los Angeles isn't too big for us to be able to find her. And this time you won't be around to butt in or do anything, except perhaps to watch until you've seen enough." He paused, then went on: "I suggest you ring her up and get her to bring those papers out here to us. She'll do it if you tell her to. Tell her that you have not been ill-treated and you'll be set free, unharmed, as soon as we get what we want."

A wide smile on his swarthy features. A regular guy.

I shook my head. "I couldn't be that deceitful," I said.

The muscles of his jaw jumped under the strain of keeping himself in check. The red flush on his face was fading into white.

"You've just made one of the biggest mistakes of your life, Merak," he said. He was in a rage, the arteries of his neck swollen into thin cords that stood out under the tanned skin. "This time you're finished. And for good."

CHAPTER THIRTEEN
ESCAPE FROM THE PARTY

Dutch meant every word he said. He got heavily to his feet, then signalled to one of his men.

"We'll give him a few hours' grace," he said. "Until morning. By that time he may have come to his senses and we'll know the whereabouts of his girlfriend. She can't have got far on foot. My guess is she jumped from the car at one of the turns. We'll soon pick her up."

"I've got plenty of men on the lookout for her," said Snow, speaking out of the corner of his mouth. He puffed nervously at his cigarette, tossing his lighter from hand to hand with quick, jumpy movements. He seemed on edge, more so than I had ever seen him before.

I wondered if Dawn had managed to slip through the cordon of men that would be stretched like a wall round Balboa, and all parts north to Los Angeles. Even if she had, where would she go? The Organisation had plenty of manpower to search fifty miles or so of road and rock.

Two of the hoodlums pulled me to my feet, grabbing my arms, and led me out into the passage to a smaller room with a single window, high up, crossed with bars of iron.

One of them stayed inside while the other went out to take up his position in the passage. They weren't taking any chances this time.

"Might as well sit down," said the tall, thin guy, indicating one of the chairs at the table. "You're not likely to be going anywhere."

I sat down; watching him narrowly. No chance of pulling anything there, even if I felt like any more rough-and-tumble games, which I didn't. I'd been through the mill enough already. Every one of my ribs ached individually.

"Just where does a guy like you fit into this deal?" I asked. Maybe if I could get him mad enough, I might get some of the answers to the questions that had been nagging at me for a long time.

Such as who had killed Maxie Temple—and why everybody had been so anxious to pin the rap on me.

"Shut up!"

"Don't you have any say in anything?" I went on, ignoring him deliberately. "Do you just do as you're told by Snow and that hoodlum McKnight?"

He grinned savagely and shifted slightly on his feet. His lips were pulled well back over his teeth.

"Don't make me kill you before I have to," he warned. There was a look in his eyes that said he'd do it if I went much further, and he'd take his chances with McKnight afterwards.

"Okay," I said. "Just relax and forget it."

He walked forward a couple of paces, still grinning, feather-balanced on the balls of his feet. "You've got one hell of a sense of humour, Merak," he muttered. "I only hope you die laughing and I'm around to see it."

The way he said it sent little chills of ice running and chasing each other up and down my spine. But I persisted, ignoring the tiny warning bell that was ringing at the back of my brain.

A cheap hoodlum who spends all his life taking orders, doing as he is told with no questions asked, living from one fear to the next, is pretty vulnerable.

Those three years in San Quentin and the four years after that waiting in bitterness for Maxie Temple to return, had taught me to think things out for myself. That was where I had the big advantage. So long as I could keep his hand away from the gun in his pocket and his itching finger off the trigger.

"Did you kill Maxie Temple?" I asked outright, hoping to evoke a shock response. I could see the startled, calculating expression leap into his eyes.

"What's the frame?" he muttered, puzzled. "You know dammed well I didn't kill him."

The same words I'd used to Snow.

"Then who did?"

"You're not in any position to ask questions. You're just a little crook who's finished." He was warming to his subject, becoming more talkative, which was what I wanted.

"Still, I don't suppose there's any harm in telling you now. Cleo Newton pulled the job. Clancy wanted

Madden to do it, but he was out of town on a job for Dutch. I knew how to do the job, but Clancy figured a dame wouldn't be spotted so easily. Besides, Temple didn't know her. He wouldn't suspect anything."

"And you knew dammed well she wouldn't talk afterwards," I said. "That was important, wasn't it? Keep her off the heroine for a little while and she'd kill anybody."

Snow had sunk to a new low with that idea, I thought. It had been like putting a loaded gun into the hands of a raving lunatic.

Poor Cleo, sunk in her own world of drugs and nightmare, living from one packet of white stuff to the next, not caring where it came from, nor how she got it, so long as it was provided regularly.

We were silent for long minutes. I looked down at my watch, but it had been smashed beyond repair in the crash. All I knew was that it was still night by the darkness outside the barred windows.

Once or twice headlights glared on the glass pane as cars swung around outside on the drive and occasionally I heard the low mutter of conversation.

It was nearly dawn as close as I could figure when the door opened and Snow came in. He looked sick; almost beaten.

"I suppose you're lucky to have a dame like that," he said, and there was a beat of sarcasm in his tone. "She must think a lot about you—I don't think."

"Just what are you talking about?"

He sat down, pulled out a cigarette, lit it and regarded

me curiously with his pale eyes. There was appraisal and something approaching pity in his stare.

"She just went to the cops. Got a lift from one of the truck drivers and spilled everything to them. Maybe she had the idea that they'd pick us up on mere suspicion. She didn't stop to think about you. All she was bothered about was her own skin. Unfortunately for either of you, she didn't have any papers or proof. They told her they couldn't do anything."

"And you made sure they didn't," I said bitterly. "They don't dare do anything without your say-so."

His eyes never left me. "That's enough, Merak," he said harshly. "I just thought I'd let you know. I think this makes your position rather precarious, to say the least. Madden arrived here less than half an hour ago. He's talking to Dutch now. I gather he's got some kind of grudge against you. For your sake, I hope Dutch doesn't hand you over to him."

Alfred Madden. The guy I'd left lying on the gravel outside Christian's. Nursing his revenge. He'd willingly kill me when he got the chance. But it would be slow and painful.

I sat there. In spite of what they said, they were getting rattled. I could sense that. Their dirty, underhand business might mean fifty million dollars to them in a year, but right now it meant only a leather envelope of papers that could stand them all in the dock.

I was glad Dawn had gone to the police and played it straight. As she saw it, it was the only thing she could do. She wasn't to know how strong was the hold these men held on Los Angeles. It hadn't taken her long to find out.

Snow edged his way out of the room and the thug came back from his position over by the door and sat down again in the chair. There was a tight, wolfish grin on his thin face. Already his finger was itching for the trigger of his gun. His eyes were narrowed to cold, bright slits. His features showed little emotion.

I sat in my chair and waited. Outside, the sky was brightening into a clear grey. I could dimly hear the dull, muffled boom of the Pacific, punctuated at odd intervals by the roar of powerful cars being driven off into the distance.

"You know what you're doing, Merak?" inquired the tall guy.

"Yes, I think so." Keep them guessing. That was my only chance now. Dawn wouldn't be standing around doing nothing; but I didn't expect much help from that quarter. She was stymied whichever way she turned.

There came a noise from the corridor outside. A muffled sound that I couldn't place. The hoodlum looked up sharply, then relaxed. He withdrew his finger from the pocket of his heavy coat and laid his hands on the table.

I had the funniest feeling that something was going to break. What it was going to be, I didn't know. But there was tension bubbling up inside me.

I stood up. The hoodlum had been watching me closely and he laughed harshly. The gun came out and he pointed it straight at me.

"Sit down," he warned. "And don't do anything stupid or I'll—"

The door opened and a well-known voice said: "Put that gun on the table, Angino, and step away, slowly."

I turned my head. Mike Spangler stood in the doorway and there was a heavy automatic in his right fist. Behind him, slumped against the wall, lay the other thug.

CHAPTER FOURTEEN
A LEATHER ENVELOPE

The tall hoodlum was wearing an expression of stupefied amazement on his chiselled features. I thought for one brief moment that he was going to use his gun and take the risk of being shot in the back, but he thought better of it and laid the weapon on the table in front of me.

Mike Spangler edged his way in. He didn't look too good. There was a bruise over his left eye and a deep cut across his left cheek, but the heavy automatic in his hand was a steady as a rock.

"An interesting situation," I said, picking up the thug's gun. He wasn't looking too pleased at the sudden turn of events. "What happened to Snow and McKnight, Mike?"

"I guess Clancy's around somewhere. Most of the others drove off in some hurry ten minutes ago. I was watching from the beach. McKnight was with them. I didn't actually see Clancy."

"Then we'd better get out of this joint while we've got the chance," I said. "I've an idea of where they're heading, and I want to beat them to it if I can. In fact, it's a matter of life and death."

"Okay, Johnny. I've got my car ready outside. What do we do with this guy?"

I made a face. "I don't like killing guys in cold blood," I replied, "but rats like this deserve it."

The thin guy's face twitched and a faint beading of sweat popped out on his forehead. He watched me steadily for a minute, and then lunged, hands outstretched and grasping, hoping to swing me around before I could press the trigger.

The heavy automatic in Mike's hand made scarcely a sound. All I did was stand back and watch him sag at the knees, doubling up as he hit the floor.

Mike and I ran out into the passage, disregarding the limp figure of the second hoodlum stretched out on the floor against the wall. He didn't move as I stepped over him, and I guessed that Mike had hit him pretty hard.

The place seemed too quiet. It had a waiting quality that tingled along my nerves. Like as not, Snow was somewhere around, but it was funny he hadn't known about Mike Spangler's arrival.

We got outside without anybody stopping us; in fact, nobody got in the way. I could feel those little nagging thoughts digging into my brain again, eating away at the edges.

Something had happened that I didn't know about. Mike Spangler, for instance. He'd helped me crack Clancy's safe, but he didn't want to run the risk of driving me back to Los Angeles. How come the sudden change of heart? Why had he, of all people, walked right into Clancy Snow's headquarters, just to rescue me?

Sure, I was his friend. And he hated Snow and the rest of his mob. But that still didn't add up to what he was doing now.

It was just beginning to get light outside. There was a kind of mist over the shore and the Pacific was a deep grey-blue, calm and flat. A few dinghies and motor-powered launches were already out a couple of miles offshore. The marlin-hunters began early in the day, before most of the others were up.

Mike's car was drawn up on the sand. Maybe that was why we hadn't heard him arrive until it was too late. The sand would have muffled the sound of the tyres, and nobody would have expected anyone to arrive from that direction. With me safe inside and the net drawing tighter around Dawn Grahame, they wouldn't be expecting anyone else.

We reached the car just as a shot echoed from the beach house. Somebody came staggering out onto the porch, aiming again in our direction.

"Keep down," hissed Mike, "unless you want to stop a bullet with your head."

"Sure," I said. I aimed a snapshot at the guy Mike had slugged earlier but he dropped back out of sight. Still no sign of the others. Had they all gone racing often to Los Angeles, hoping to ransack Dawn's place and find the envelope? It seemed the only likely explanation.

Another shot from the tired-looking stucco façade,

this time nearer, more accurate. It smashed off the front wing of the car. Then he made a mistake and came out into the open, thinking he had us pinned down. It was his last mistake. Mike's bullet struck him full in the chest, spinning him round, knocking him back against the woodwork.

"Let's beat them to the punch, Mike," I said urgently. "We'll get to Los Angeles before they do if we take the 101 Highway." I didn't even convince myself, but it was something to say.

Mike laughed softly. "Don't kid yourself, Johnny. But we'll die trying."

The car purred, tyres tore at the sand, spewing it high into the air, then got a grip and spun us forward. A minute later we found the road and the speedometer needle crept up through the fifties as a Mike put his foot down on the accelerator.

I looked down at the beach house, quiet in the light of dawn, and hoped fervently that I wouldn't see the place again unless it was with a couple of dozen Federal men at my back, ready to blast the rats out of the hole.

It had certainly been a nice quiet place in which to die. If it hadn't been for Mike, I most likely would have died.

The highway was deserted for the first dozen miles or so. Balboa came and went and we hit the cloverleaf intersection just outside Newport at fifty. The sun popped up while we were still some twenty-six miles from Los Angeles.

I lit a cigarette and watched Mike as he concentrated

on the road ahead.

"Something worrying you, Johnny?" he asked, sensing me watching him.

"One or two things," I replied. "Particularly why you risked your neck to get me out of that place. Don't tell me you were taking such a risk just for an old friend."

He sucked in his cheeks, his face set. "That would have been pretty insane, wouldn't it?"

"It would. So I figured you must have some other reason, though I can't quite see it at the moment."

We overtook a couple of north-bound trucks, hauling their loads of tuna from the canning factories of Balboa. At that moment I would gladly have exchanged places with either of the drivers, whoever they were.

Mike spoke slowly: "I had to do that back there, Johnny. Not for you or even for myself, but for someone else. I didn't know about her until last night. I saw it in those papers you took from Snow's safe. But I still had to be sure. For the past five or six I've been the smart guy. Staying out of trouble, hiding away in Balboa, staying alive and hoping I'd stay that way, keeping away from contacts with men like Snow and McKnight. But I was only kidding myself. I must have been stupid, but I damn well see it now. They had to have something to hold against me. To make me jump when they wanted me to."

He paused and after a few minutes of silence between us, I said: "It was Cleo Newton, wasn't it?"

Mike nodded. Funny I had never guessed.

"Cleo," he said. There was a depth of meaning in

that single word, the way he said it. He looked at me sideways for a long moment and his face got tired and old. Then he said by way of explanation: "She was a damned nice kid before she got mixed up with people like Alfred Madden. I didn't know about that, or I'd have killed him in the very beginning. Then all this might never have happened."

"And I might be dead now, Mike."

"Sorry, Johnny, I didn't mean it that way."

"Sure, I know." I nodded. "Go on."

"Cleo Newton, she's my niece," he said wearily. His voice sounded as though it had been drained of all hope. "When her father and mother died, I brought her up as best I could. It wasn't much of a life for her, so I guess I'm really responsible for what happened. I didn't give her what she needed most. Security. Always moving around from one place to another. So she went off with some crumb of a musician and his band in one of the joints in Los Angeles. I couldn't stop her—she was over twenty-one.

"It seemed all right then, but it must have been while she was singing at that nightclub that she first met up with Madden, and—" He broke off. His white-knuckled hands gripped the wheel convulsively.

"—and started to take drugs," I finished it for him.

"That's right." I'd never seen a man so changed within a few short hours. He'd been scared before; now he was broken, but angry.

I hoped he would catch up with Madden sometime in the future, if only for Cleo Newton's sake. A kid who'd got off to a bad start when she'd met up with something she didn't quite understand—something exciting.

Perhaps she and I were two of a kind. Wanting to be big. Trying to get into the swim with the others. Playing it big. Cleo Newton starting on the drug craze because it had seemed dangerously exciting at first, giving no thought to what would come after. Me, Johnny Merak, acting tough because all the other kids on the block did the same.

Mike fell silent and I didn't question him any further. There were some things a man likes to keep to himself, and one on them was murder when he felt it in his heart.

We neared Los Angeles and I had that feeling inside me that we'd lost the race. Snow and McKnight would have reached their destination by now. But the leather envelope was well hidden. Even with a squad of men, it would take them several hours to find it unless they struck it pretty lucky.

But what was happening to Dawn all this time? Had she gone back to her place or was she still hanging around the local precinct, trying to convince the police of the truth of what she was saying. If that really was the case, she was simply wasting her time.

"You got any ideas that'll help us when we get there?" asked Mike harshly, as we ran through the suburbs of Los Angeles.

"No."

"From what I've been able to gather, you're in a bad jam, Johnny."

"I'll think of something."

"Maybe. But don't make it any harder on yourself than it is already."

I didn't say anything to that; there wasn't really anything to say. All my life, unconsciously perhaps, I'd been making things harder for myself. The trouble was, I didn't know it at the time.

Little things are tallied up over the years. A spot of fixing here, blackmail there, a crooked deal of an election. Things like that.

There had been terror in those days, but it had all been on the other side, it hadn't affected me personally. It did now. We turned into the quiet, residential district where Dawn lived.

Two sleek Cadillacs were drawn up in array against the kerb, their drivers behind the wheel of each machine. The house looked ominously quiet behind the well-kept garden and the drawn curtains.

McKnight was here. Snow was here; and the big machine that was the Underworld Organisation was rolling in fast to smash the puny opposition of Johnny Merak. I knew, instinctively, that this was no time for subtle or roundabout tactics. It had to be done fast and decisively.

"Stop the car at the corner, Mike," I said tensely. "I'm going in there after them."

"Sure, Johnny. I'm in," he said, switching off the ignition. "But leave Madden for me."

"You'll get him, Mike," I promised, "but not this time. I need you here in the car, ready for a quick take-off. They may have Dawn in there and if we come out running, I'll need you ready."

I didn't like slapping him in the face like that, smashing his hopes. But it had to be done whether I liked it or not. There was more at stake here than Mike Spangler and Alfred Madden, much more.

"If I see him, I'll kill him, Johnny." There was a taut insistence in his low voice. His fingers twitched nervously. "So help me if I don't."

There was no sense in sitting there arguing with him in that mood. I could see the point he was trying to make. If I'd been in his place, I'd have done the same.

I got out of the car, stretched my aching limbs and checked the clip in my .38.

"Keep your eyes open, Mike, and be ready in case I come running."

He nodded. A little guy with a lot of bitterness and revenge that had to be worked out of his system.

"You must be insane to go busting in there alone."

"Can you suggest anything better?"

"No. But I still think you're crazy. They'll drop you before you get through the door."

I started walking, circling the block. It would have to be the back entrance if I was to stand anything of a chance at all. The iron-grilled gate, set in the stone wall, was closed with a lock and chain.

With an effort that wrenched my shoulder muscles I swung myself over the wall and landed in the soft earth of the garden. If they had anybody posted at the rear windows I was finished; but I was banking everything on them thinking I was still tucked away safely at the beach house over forty miles away. The element of surprise was still mine, but it was only a slim advantage.

I reached the back door, turned the handle gently, easily. It swung open and I slipped inside. Then I stopped.

Clancy Snow's voice reached me, speaking from one of the rooms.

CHAPTER FIFTEEN
CLANCY CRIES MURDER

"It's got to be around here someplace. That guy never left his house all day until he headed out for Balboa. Tear down the whole place if you have too, but find it. And hurry! We haven't got all day."

Some other guy laughed at that. It was the sound of a concrete mixer grinding at little chips of marble. A chair crashed to the floor. I heard Snow swearing softly and continuously under his breath.

A tall, blond guy came blundering out of the big room, heading for the kitchen. He never even turned his head to look at me. The first he knew about it was when I cracked him over the head with the butt of the .38. He made plenty of noise as he hit the floor, but I wasn't caring about silence.

"Hey! What the hell's going on out there?" Madden's voice from the big room. He was coming towards the door as I stepped inside, levelling the gun at him.

"Stay quite still, everybody," I said. "You're not going anywhere."

Snow stood in the middle of the room. It looked as though he had seen a ghost. His jaw had dropped and he was swallowing visibly, trying to get the words out. Behind him, McKnight turned slowly. There was hate in his eyes as well as puzzled surprise. He moved his right hand towards a pocket of his coat, stopped as the .38 swung a little in his direction.

"I don't propose to ask how you managed to get away," said Dutch slowly, deliberately.

"Get over against the wall, all of you," I said sharply. I held the advantage now, but for how long? At any moment either of the two gorillas in the cars outside might take it into his head to come barging in, spoiling everything.

They obeyed the order reluctantly. Madden looked at me as though daring me to relax for one single second. I knew he'd shoot me the minute I turned my gaze from him.

"A pity some of you guys don't like coffee," I said, taking the lid off the big can on the table. "It's good for you."

I took out the slim leather envelope and slipped it carefully in my inside pocket. Snow said something unintelligible between his clenched teeth. McKnight simply looked at me, but there was the promise of death in his eyes.

"You'll regret this, Merak," said McKnight. He spoke without heat, but with a terrible intensity in his voice.

"Somehow I don't think so," I said. "The trouble with you, McKnight, is that you think like a crook. You don't believe that it's possible for a guy to get so fed up with this business that he'll do anything to feel clean again. I haven't been able to look any decent-living citizen in the face for ten years without feeling dirty and ashamed. Starting now, I'm going to change all that."

"You'll never change, Johnny," said Snow as I backed towards the door. "If you are not entirely satisfied with the way the Organisation has treated you in the past, just say so, and we're willing to arrange things to suit you. A substantial position—" he was pleading with me now, watching all his dreams, his empire, slipping away with the envelope in my pocket. "We'll forget all that's happened in the past, clear you of all the murder raps set out against you."

"Can you ever make me feel really clean again?" I asked.

"You're making a mistake—a big mistake," said McKnight.

"Could be," I said. "But in case any of you guys want to be a hero and come running after me, I wouldn't. It isn't worth it."

I backed out of the door, watching them all, not focusing my gaze on anything in particular, so as to take in every little detail. None of them moved. If I knew Madden, however, he'd stick so close to me from now on he'd be walking in my shadow.

I slammed the back door as one of the men came rushing out into the passage. His first slug splintered through the wood above my head.

Then I was running for the bottom of the garden, the

gun tight in my hand. I took a jump at the wall, levered myself up on my hands and got my legs on top. There was a faint plop behind me and a stone block a few inches from my hand spat into fragments as the bullet kicked into it.

Frantically, I thrashed my legs, rolled over, landed on the sidewalk and started running. I'd made about twenty yards when I looked back and saw a head appear over the top of the wall. Instinctively, I lengthened my stride and began to zigzag. Another bullet hummed over my head. They were coming up fast. As I made the corner of the block, I looked back again. Madden and another man were racing along the sidewalk less than thirty yards behind.

I turned into the wider road and saw Mike's car ahead of me. The engine was ticking over as I slipped inside.

"Step on it, Mike," I said breathlessly. "There's a whole hornet's nest behind me."

He threw in the clutch without asking any questions, just as Madden and the other guy raced into sight at the corner of the block, expressions of awful determination written all over their faces.

My nerves were screaming deep inside me as they started shooting. They had to stop us now.

Somewhere in the distance I heard the roar of powerful cars. Snow had lost no time in getting out front.

A slug smashed into the windscreen as we passed the two hoodlums on the corner. There was a pained expression on Mike's face as he saw Madden slip away in the distance behind us. I knew what he was thinking and I felt sorry for him.

"Where to?" Mike's voice was dry and toneless.

"The nearest Federal Office," I said. "And hurry! They're on our tail already."

They were; but Mike seemed to know a lot about the streets of Los Angeles. He must have had a roadmap for a brain from the way he hurled the car about, doubling back on himself half a dozen times.

Action was the only answer now. In my pocket I carried a slim leather envelope packed with political dynamite. Unless I wanted it to blow up in my face, I had to get it into the right hands at once.

Mike found the place we were looking for and parked the car outside. Opening the door, I ran up the steps, having left my gun behind in the car with Mike.

I'd heard of the guy in the office on the third floor. He was a good man; perhaps the only one I could reach at a moment's notice and know that he wasn't in the pay of Snow and his crowd. He wouldn't be bought and, being a Federal man, he wasn't scared easily.

His name was Harry Grenville, and I had to get to him quick.

Mr. Grenville was in, said the secretary at the desk, had I the usual appointment?"

"My name's Merak," I said hurriedly. "And this is urgent. I didn't have either the time or the opportunity to make an appointment."

She hesitated, then pressed a switch on the panel in

front of her. Maybe she had me figured for some political screwball, but she'd give me a try. A man's voice answered.

"Yes?"

"A gentleman to see you, Mr. Grenville. He hasn't an appointment, but he says it's important."

"Urgent!" I said.

"All right. Send him in and see that we're not disturbed."

She seemed to find a new interest in me after that and showed me to the door at the far end of the corridor. Knocking, we went inside.

"Mr. Merak?" he said quietly. Then I was inside and face-to-face with the guy I'd been trying to see for a long time.

Harry Grenville was seated behind a mahogany desk, but he rose to his feet as I walked forward and waved me to a chair. He was not smiling and it was difficult to imagine a face like that smiling very often.

"You wanted to see me concerning something important, I believe my secretary said, Mr. Merak."

I nodded. "I've something here that I think might be of interest to you," I said. "I'd have taken it to the police, but it's just possible they might be taking orders from the men I'm trying to expose."

"I'm afraid I don't understand." He looked puzzled.

"With this evidence you'll be able to bust the Clancy Snow Organisation wide open."

He picked up his ears at the mention of Clancy Snow. And there was surprise on his face.

"You've got something concrete on him?" A harsh voice with disbelief in it. "I've been trying for two years but I've never been able to pin anything on him so that it would stick."

I took out the envelope, threw it onto his desk. "Take a look at the private papers of Snow and Dutch McKnight," I said. "Then tell me whether you've got anything definite."

He gave me another look, then opened the envelope and laid the papers on the top of the desk. His eyebrows went up as he began to read through them. When he had finished, he gave me an incredulous whistle, laid them down, and nodded his head.

"I don't know how you managed to get your hands on these," he said, "but they're dynamite."

"You'll have to hurry up if you want to pick them up," I reminded him. "If I know Snow, we'll have to prise him out of a mountain of artillery."

I was feeling better now, more relaxed. For good or evil, it was done. I had almost finished what I had set out to do.

"You know where these men can be located?"

"I've a pretty good idea. They'll know by now that the Federal Authorities have got these documents and that they have lost their pitch. Unless I miss my guess, they're running back to their hideout at Balboa. After that, unless we move, they'll be over the border into Mexico like Maxie Temple seven years ago."

"I'm beginning to get the idea." He spoke quickly into the communicator on his desk, then flicked the switch back into place. "It'll have to be quick and rough," he said, pausing to look up at me again. "I've called in some men. These papers were all I need to act. We have got them where we want them even if, as you say, we have got to dig them out of their hole."

"Can you get any line on a girl named Dawn Grahame for me?" I asked. "She called at one of the precincts and tried to tip them off about this, but without papers, she didn't stand a chance. She was just hitting her head against a brick wall with Snow sitting on the top."

"I think I understand what you're getting at." Harry Grenville wasn't the kind of man who allowed false sentiment to blind him to what was really going on. "I'll put a call through for you. Meanwhile, you'd better come with us. We may need you. Have you got a car outside?"

"Sure," I said. "And an extra man. He wants to be in at the kill if possible. I'll explain if you like, but it's to do with a girl named Cleo Newton."

"More names," said Grenville. He was smiling now from the first time. A tight-lipped smile that did nothing to his face. "Was this Cleo Newton a friend of his?"

"Yes, his niece."

"So? Okay, bring him along, too. But there's likely to be some shooting, so warn him to watch himself. That goes for you, too, Merak."

There was a buzz on the instrument in front of him. Grenville flicked across a switch. "Yes?"

I couldn't hear what the secretary at the other end said for the sound of sirens wailing in the street outside.

But it was obviously the call he'd been expecting. He nodded his head, then stood up quickly. "Let's move," he said, and started for the door like a piece of lubricated lightning. Rarely had I seen a man of his size move so fast outside of a boxing booth.

Outside, Mike was sitting tight with half a dozen big convertibles surrounding him. He looked up at me as I slipped into the seat beside him.

"For a minute, I thought you hadn't got away with it, and they'd come for Jonny Merak, smart guy who's landed himself in trouble again."

"Relax, Mike," I said. "I've talked Grenville into it. We're moving out to Balboa, and this time we're going to flush those rats out of that beach house before they know what's hit them."

"Good work, Johnny." He jabbed the self-starter, eased the car gently away from the kerb. Grenville opened the rear door and eased his bulky frame inside.

"I guess I'll stick around with you fellas," he said with that tight grin I'd seen before. "This is beginning to get more and more interesting every minute."

Out of Los Angeles and heading south, a single file of sleek convertibles behind us, strung out at regular intervals. I wondered what Snow was doing right now. Sweating ice-cubes, trying to figure out my moves, knowing that he hadn't any more aces up his sleeve.

Dawn was well out of his reach and retribution was moving in fast. Traffic wasn't too heavy and we were able to make good time. Whenever we ran into a stream of heavy trucks, the sirens on the cars behind us cleared the way. Trucks and cars backed into the roadside and slowly fell behind.

"Now suppose you sketch in the picture for me, Merak?" said Grenville from the back seat. There was little curiosity in his deep voice, but a note of authority made me realise that it would be more than stupid to hold anything back.

"I've been working in this sewer that Snow's built up in Los Angeles over the past ten years. Before that it was Maxie Temple. Everything this side of sheer cold-blooded murder came easy. It wasn't until Temple was shot that I decided to do something about it. I wanted to get out, stay clean, but first I had to get hold of some papers that Temple was holding over me. I thought I'd be able to get to him when he arrived in Los Angeles and force him to return them, but after he was shot I realised Snow must have picked them up."

"So you decided to go after them yourself instead of coming to us?"

"What use would it have been to come to you? Without evidence it would only have been my word against Snow's, and as far as you are concerned he was a regular guy, well thought of in civic circles. As for me, a no-good crook, what chance would I have had?"

"Okay, go on. So you went after these papers. What then?"

"I got Mike here to help me bust Snow's safe out at Balboa. That's where I found the papers."

"When was this?"

"A couple of nights ago."

"Then why didn't you bring them to me then? I suppose you know I could charge you for withholding evidence?"

"Sure! But if I'd done that, they'd have killed Dawn Grahame. They managed to pick her up and brought out to this beach house."

"Apparently, you have been mixed up in some pretty shady business. I'm glad, though, you decided to be frank with me. I'll see what I can do to help you. You have done me a great service. Besides, I understand from my records that you have already spent three years in San Quentin; and these papers prove you were innocent of that charge."

There was little conversation after that. Mike concentrated on his driving. Grenville seemed absorbed in some private problem of his own, while I was too busy thinking about Dawn, wondering where she was, what she was doing.

Nine-thirty. We ran through the streets of Balboa at a steady fifty. There was a cluster of local police cars at the big intersection, and I guess that word had already gone ahead, burning along the wires, notifying every officer in that area that Clancy Snow and Dutch McKnight were wanted on a Federal charge.

"Pull into the side," ordered Grenville as I spotted the cars.

Mike obeyed, gliding the car into the kerb. One of the officers walked forward.

"You were right, Mr. Grenville," he said, peering into the rear of the car. "They headed this way less than half an hour ago. Like you said, we didn't stop them. There's another roadblock the other side of Balboa. They can't get out now unless they decide to swim for it."

"Or unless they've got a powerful launch at the beach house," I said, thinking aloud. "I didn't spot any, but it's just possible."

"My God, you're right!" Grenville nodded. "I'd better call in the patrol boats and see if you can get a helicopter, just in case. We'll try to head them off at the beach house."

"Very good, Mr. Grenville."

People on the sidewalks stared after as we drove along the promenade. This was something new, but they couldn't guess at the real importance behind it. They'd have had to be in from the very beginning to know that.

Grenville took a small automatic from his pocket, checked it mechanically, then leaned forward over the seat. "This is likely to get tough," he warned. "I'll see about getting you both a couple of guns. Clancy Snow will do his best to take you with him for this."

I lit a cigarette. My eyes were like grit and my chest seemed on fire every time I drew in a breath. Up ahead, the beach house, standing alone on its rising knoll of ground looked deserted.

I looked out to sea, but there was nothing in sight apart from the usual marlin-hunters, far out on the horizon.

CHAPTER SIXTEEN
THE END OF THE LINE

The deserted nature of the beach house lasted until we were within a hundred yards of it. Then it came alive. It was perhaps the way that the curtains had been drawn aside slightly at each window facing the road that rang an alarm bell in my mind and activated my reflexes. I had an impression of men waiting behind those windows with guns in their hands, waiting for us to get within striking distance.

I saw all that in the fraction of a second before I pressed Mike's foot down hard on the brake and spun the wheel sharply to the left.

The car stopped, hurling us forward against the dash as a hail of bullets splashed against the windscreen. Grenville was cursing steadily in the back of the car. Whether he had anticipated the move was difficult to tell, but the bullets had droned within inches of his head before striking the rear of the car.

The other cars had stopped a little distance behind and men were climbing out, heads well down, feet sinking into the sand. Gingerly, I eased myself upright. No sign that another fusillade of shots was on the way, but it was still dangerous to stay where we were.

Swinging open the door, I crawled out head-first, jumped for the cover of a tall palm tree, and waited while Mike and Grenville came panting up beside me.

"It didn't take them long to draw that bead on us," said Mike. "How are we going to get near enough to run them out?"

"Leave that to me," said Grenville. He waved a couple of men forward. They carried tear gas guns in their hands. Grenville pointed towards the upper windows of the beach house, then motioned them down, ready.

Another guy came running up, doubled over, carrying a megaphone. He handed it to Grenville.

"Can you hear me in there, Snow?" Grenville's voice boomed out of the loudspeaker. "This is your last chance to surrender; if not, we're coming in there after you."

"Come in and try your luck, punk." Albert Madden's voice. I saw the tightness come to Mike's face and felt him stiffen as he crouched beside me. His fingers crept into his inside pocket, closing about the gun.

"Very well, if you want it the hard way."

Grenville handed the megaphone back to the officer and gave the order to open fire on the place. Everybody was watching the place now. Two of the men moved forward under cover of fire from behind.

It was as though it had all been planned out before-hand. A couple of tear gas bombs were lobbed expertly into the upper windows. There came the faint tinkle of breaking glass, followed by the writhing of white smoke through the smashed panes.

"That ought to fetch some of them out," said Grenville. His mouth was set and the muscles of his jaw lumped.

All that Mike and I did was to stand clear. Five, perhaps six, of the men that rushed forward, firing as they went. Three of them worked their way around the back of the house, disappearing from sight.

I saw one of the thugs, leaning from an upper window, screaming at the top of his voice. He flung his gun away and was clawing at his face. Tear gas built up at his back.

It was a busy fight while it lasted, which was maybe half an hour.

Slowly, the hail of bullets from the beach house diminished until there was little more than a desultory shot fired in our direction. None of Grenville's men looked worried or excited.

"Okay, I think we can go in now, but watch yourself." Grenville looked round at me, his eyebrows lifted.

I walked forward over the sand with Mike Spangler at my heels. I could guess what kind of thoughts were running through his head. He was hoping that somehow Madden was still alive in there, and that he'd be the first to run up against him.

I saw him take the automatic out of his pocket as we approached the porch. One of Snow's hoods lay face downwards in the sand, his body propped against the woodwork almost ludicrously.

We stepped over him after paying him a cursory

glance. There was blood on his chest and he obviously wasn't going to take any more interest in what was going on around him.

On the stairs we ran into the tear gas making its way down. The place seemed quiet, but there was a peculiar waiting quality again that I didn't like. If only I had been able to put my finger on it, I wouldn't have felt so bad.

Grenville was a dark figure striding ahead, taking no chances, his gun ready, eyes alert. Other men were moving around on the stairs, coughing as the gas got into the lungs.

Two men came down the stairs carrying a limp body between them. As they passed me I looked down and found myself staring into the still face of Clancy Snow. He was dead because he couldn't believe in defeat and he wanted to be there at the very moment of triumph.

I walked slowly into the room at the back where we'd been kept prisoner earlier. The table was still there in the middle of the room and the two chairs placed neatly around. The place was a shambles, however, apart from that.

I didn't hear the door close gently behind me until Madden's voice said: "You, Merak. Turn round slowly so that I can see your face before you die."

He had a gun in his hand. I knew that before I turned. He was standing behind the door, watching me with hate in his eyes.

"I've been waiting for this for a long time," he said, lips drawn back across his teeth. "I warned you before that I'd kill you. Well, this is it."

His grin widened and the knuckles of his hand whitened as he exerted pressure on the trigger. I tensed myself for the impact of the bullet, but it never came.

There was a crack of the silencer in his hand, but the bullet ploughed a neat furrow into the wall behind me as the door opened sharply, hitting Madden in the small of the back, pitching him forward.

I reached instinctively for the .38 in my pocket, but it wasn't necessary. Mike Spangler backed into the room. His face was twisted with hate.

Madden straightened, but I kicked the gun from his fingers. Spangler was walking forward, his eyes bright lines in his face.

"Do you know me?"

Madden looked at him in sudden surprise, then puzzlement. "What's with you?" he asked.

"Very soon, Madden, you're going to die, but I want you to know who's pulled the trigger that sends you into eternity. Perhaps you remember Cleo Newton. You took her away from me over eight years ago.

"I've only just discovered what you have done to her in that time, Madden. Now I'm going to repay you for everything."

"But what she got to do with you?" Madden, like the coward he was, was screaming now. Fear showed on his face.

"Cleo Newton was my niece." Mike pulled the trigger and Madden stumbled forward onto his face.

When Grenville came back he didn't ask any

awkward questions, though I guessed he knew quite a lot.

"Any of them still alive?" I asked, as we walked back to the car.

"A couple. We got Dutch McKnight. He was pretty badly wounded, but we expect him to live. He'll be in hospital for a couple of months, then he'll stand his trial."

"And the others?" Mike looked interested.

"They're finished. I think with the evidence we have in this envelope we ought to be able to clear up most of the mess in Los Angeles. There are probably some we can't touch, but the big ones are finished."

We drove the forty miles or so back to Los Angeles and the three of us in the car were quiet. My body still felt as though it had been dropped from a plane and my clothes were sticking to my skin with sweat.

But that didn't matter now. The first time since I can remember, I could hold up my head and feel clean and respectable.

"What are you going to do now, Johnny?" It was the first time anyone like Grenville had called me by my first name.

"I don't know. Try to get a decent job, I reckon. If anybody will have me. There isn't much I can do, but I'll try."

"You might make a good detective if you only put your mind to it," said Grenville pleasantly. "You seem to know all the angles, even if you had to be on the wrong side of the law to learn them. It might come in useful. I could use somebody like you."

"Sure." I laughed although my face was aching all over. "How much does a job like that pay, assuming you stay alive to collect?"

"About two hundred a week."

"I'll take it," I said.

"What about this girl of yours—Dawn Grahame, isn't it?"

"I don't know. That's something I haven't thought about for a long time."

We dropped Grenville off at his office, then went on to Dawn's place, just in case she'd arrived back while we'd been away. I'd half-expected a news item over the police radios, but there had been nothing, so perhaps they were still checking.

"I think I'll be getting along," said Mike, as we reached the house. "It's getting late, and all this excitement isn't good for me at my age."

I laughed. It was good to laugh again and think that for once I was quits with the world.

"Sure, Mike," I said. "I'll be seeing you."

"Sure, Johnny." I watched him ease the car away. A little guy, but with all the bitterness burned out of him. He'd faced a lot these past few hours, like somebody walking a dangerously thin rope, but finally he'd reached the end of it.

I didn't have any of the answers as far as Dawn was concerned. I let myself in and called her name.

No answer.

I went into the big room. Someone had been there

because the table had been righted, but I couldn't see her.

I went out into the passage. There was a smell of coffee coming from the kitchen. Dawn was standing there with her back to me as I walked in.

She didn't turn until I got my arms around her, then she smiled up at me.

Her voice was soft. There was a sparkle beginning to come back into her eyes, but the little devil seemed to have dropped out of sight and been drowned long ago in the depths together with the fire and the hunger; and the gates to her private hell had been sealed at last.

"I'd guessed you'd come back here, Johnny."

"I had to," I said simply. "There was nowhere else to go."

She smiled again. "I said before that you were one hell of a guy. But there's still something about you I can't get out of my system."

"I grow on people that way," I said, "particularly dark-haired women who make a point of getting guys out of trouble."

We went into the big room and sat down at the table, with the rest of the room scattered in disorder around us.

"By the way," I said, "Grenville, the Federal guy, offered me a job if I cared to take it."

"Oh, what sort of job?"

"He seemed to have some funny idea that I'd make a good cop," I said. "Imagine me, Johnny Merak, ex-crook, turning cop."

She was silent for almost a minute. Then she said: "Well, why not? It's as good a job as any, I suppose."

"I guess so." I was feeling more human now. "It's hard to explain, but I found out today that the only thing lying at the end of racketeering and threats and violence is more violence, and you never come out on top in the end."

"What happened to Clancy Snow and the others?"

"Snow's dead. Dutch McKnight was wounded in the gun battle, but he's on his way to a hospital now. They think he'll live to stand his trial."

"So that's it?"

"Yes, Dawn. Clancy's world crashed about him this morning out at Balboa Bay. It never seemed to have entered his head that he would lose out on the deal. He had everything sewn up and in his pocket except Grenville."

"And Johnny Merak, who started it all," said Dawn, quietly.

"I guess I don't count for much," said. "I couldn't do much by myself."

"But you have got the chance you wanted now, Johnny. Take it and don't let it slip out of your grasp this time as it did ten years ago."

I drank my coffee. It wasn't quite as easy as that. How many more Clancy Snows or Dutch McKnights were there in Los Angeles, waiting to blow up in the face of the community?

But for a woman who had faith in me when I needed it most, I might have been one of them, boiling up inside, hoping to take over from the Big Men who had been toppled from their pedestals.

But I could forget that now. That was all past and finished with. I went over to the window and looked out. Some kids were playing ball in the street.

"Funny," I said, "but Los Angeles seems a lot cleaner today. Maybe it's because I feel that way myself."

Dawn smiled over her shoulder as she went back into the kitchen.

"Maybe it really is a lot cleaner," she said.

ABOUT THE AUTHOR

JOHN STEPHEN GLASBY was born in 1928, and graduated from Nottingham University with an honours degree in Chemistry. He started his career as a research chemist for I.C.I. in 1952, and worked for them until his retirement. Over the next two decades, he began a parallel career as an extraordinarily prolific writer of science fiction novels and short stories, his first novels appearing in the summer of 1952 from Curtis Warren Ltd. under various house pseudonyms such as "Rand Le Page" and "Berl Cameron," as was the fashion of the day. Late in 1952, he began an astonishing association with the London publisher, John Spencer Ltd., which was to last more than twenty years.

Glasby quickly became Spencer's main author, writing hundreds of stories and novels on commissions in several genres. Not only was Glasby required to switch back and forth from science fiction to supernatural stories (his preferred media), but also to Foreign Legion sagas, Second World War novels, hospital romances, crime novels, and westerns. He quickly amassed a large number of personal pseudonyms, the best known being "A. J. Merak," under which name a number of his science fiction novels were reprinted in the 1960s in the United States.

When his association with John Spencer eventually ended, he took the opportunity to sell a science fiction novel under his own name to Don Wollheim at Ace Books (*Project Jove*, 1971). Always a great fan of the work of H. P. Lovecraft, he then wrote a collection of Mythos stories for August Derleth at Arkham House. Derleth suggested extensive revisions and improvements, which Glasby duly followed, but then unfortunately died before the collection could be published, and the book was returned.

Interested in astronomy since childhood, Glasby had joined the variable star section of the British Astronomical Society in 1958, and was made Director in 1965. He was elected a Fellow of the Royal Astronomical Society in 1960, and he published numerous textbooks and encyclopedias on astronomy and chemistry, the first being *Variable Stars* in 1968.

During the early 1960s, Glasby wrote dozens of paperback westerns, all of which were reprinted in hardcover and paperback four decades later. Their success prompted the author to write new westerns, of which almost a dozen have appeared in recent years. Also revived were his 1960s "Johnny Merak" private eye novels, and Glasby continued to write new adventures of his Chandler-like hero.

Following his retirement from I.C.I., Glasby returned to writing more supernatural stories in the Lovecraftian vein, and a number of his stories have appeared in American small press magazines and in Mythos anthologies edited by Robert M. Price. In recent years new supernatural stories have appeared in original collections edited by leading horror anthologist Stephen Jones, and in Philip Harbottle's *Fantasy Adventures* collections (published by Wildside Press).

His novelette, "Innsmouth Bane," was featured in the second issue of *H. P. Lovecraft's Magazine of Horror*. Glasby's most ambitious Lovecraftian work was *Dark Armageddon*, as yet unpublished, a trilogy of novels that unifies and brings to a climatic conclusion Lovecraft's Cthulhu Mythos cycle.

An all-new collection of ghost stories, *The Substance of a Shade*, was published in the UK in 2003, followed by *The Dark Destroyer*, a new supernatural novel, in 2005. In 2007 Glasby was adjudged the ideal choice to continue John Russell Fearn's famous "Golden Amazon" series, and three authorized novels, *Seetee Sun*, *The Sun Movers*, and *The Crimson Peril*, have appeared to date. A fourth novel, *Primordial World*, is scheduled to appear in 2012.

Several of the best of Glasby's SF, supernatural, and detective titles are being published by the Borgo Press.

John Glasby died on June 5, 2011, following a long and courageous battle with illness, during which time he continued to write with undimmed power.